BETRAYAL IN THE CAPITOL

B. IVY WOODS

BRETAGEY PRESS

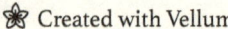

To Ivy,

For keeping me sane.

1

Juliana 'Jules' Cartwright glared at her reflection as she dried her hands. She had plenty of other things she needed to worry about and right now wasn't the time to get emotional. After pulling it out of her purse, she reapplied her red lipstick that she'd put on right after work. A quick shake of her hair helped to liven up the current state of her mood, which was all over her face. She straightened her spine and squared her shoulders, preparing to take on whatever would be thrown at her the rest of the night, and walked out of the bathroom with her head held high.

Another night, another fundraiser she had to smile her way through on behalf of the Cartwright Foundation. At least she wasn't alone because her father was also attending, but sometimes when they would get split up, she was left to fend for herself. This was not to say that she couldn't do so but having to be 'on' all the time did end up being a pain in the ass. What kept her going was that the projects they were funding were for good causes.

The lightly veiled comments about how she looked or how much she had changed since the last time they had seen her were annoying, but it went beyond just that. The look in their eyes would tell her what their words truly meant—disgusting her further. Most of the comments were made on the sly, probably because they didn't want to offend her father versus caring about her feelings. After all, they didn't want to hurt the relationships they had built with her father because, in some ways, he held the strings to the purse that could fund some of the endeavors they may try to pursue in the future.

The Cartwright Foundation's reputation had been built over decades of hard work. Her grandfather started it years ago and passed it down to her father, William, when he retired. Once William had taken the reins, he took the foundation to new heights, and Jules hoped that at some point in the future she'd be able to take over. Although she did have a brother who also could have a stake in the foundation, if he wanted to, he'd shown no interest, instead choosing to focus on his interests in the tech industry.

With a sigh, she put on a fake polite smile as she walked past some of the people she knew, acknowledging them as she crossed the room to her father. It was clear that he was in deep conversation with the man to his left. None of this was unusual at these types of events. Everyone wanted a piece of the money and backing that the Cartwrights could offer.

Sometimes, Jules felt as if this was her only purpose. Show up to these gatherings, schmooze with these people who probably couldn't care less about anything outside of money, and head home. A yawn escaped her lips before she could stop it. The closer she got to her father, the more intrigued she was by the conversation he was having. Something about the man rubbed her the wrong way. She knew that she shouldn't judge someone based on appearances, but the way that her father was standing, guarded with his arms crossed, told her otherwise.

Upon making it back to her father's side, he smiled at her before returning to his conversation that she didn't want to interrupt. She could tell he was trying to wrap up the discussion, but the man in the dark brown suit was refusing to let him go. That wasn't uncommon either. They figured the more they could talk his ear off, the higher the likelihood it was they would get what they wanted. It was almost laughable because William Cartwright wasn't known to cower to anyone.

Jules was grateful she didn't get pulled into the conversation with her father and this mystery man. Instead, her eyes danced over the venue as she wondered how much longer she had to stay, because her couch was calling her name. Relaxing in front of her television with a slice of the chocolate cake she'd brought on a whim the other day was the motivation that would get her through the rest of this event. Her eyes moved over the crowd and stalled when they landed the last person she wanted to see.

In walked Garrett West, who'd just followed his father, Terry, into the room. It took everything in her not to throw a glare his way. Jules couldn't stand the sight of him, let alone being in the same room as him. When his eyes met hers, she stopped breathing for a moment. It took everything in her to hold back her true feelings in public. It had been years since Jules had seen him, outside of when he had crashed happy hour with her friends, and she preferred it that way. Now this was the second time that she'd found herself in the same room as him. That was too much.

When his eyes didn't shift from hers, an involuntary shiver ran down her back, and Jules did everything in her power to stop any movement which might have resembled the tremble that slid through her body. He didn't seem to be as surprised to see her as she was to see him.

The way Garrett looked in his suit put all of the men in the room to shame. The black formal wear caressed his body, as if it were made specifically with him in mind. Although she couldn't see their color from here, Jules could feel his blue eyes caressing her curves ever so softly, as if he was studying every inch of her through the black dress she was wearing. Part of Jules hoped to keep her attention on him inconspicuous, but it was just her luck that both Garrett and Terry were making their way toward her and her father.

When the two men reached the father-daughter duo, the man who William was speaking with scurried away, and Jules watched as her father straightened his shoulders and turned to bestow a bright smile at the new arrivals. "Terry, great to see you."

Terry stuck his hand out to shake William's. "Same, and the same to you, Jules. I think the last time was when..."

"Gladys invited Carol and me over for dinner a few months ago," William completed Terry's sentence for him.

"That's right! Time is flying and I can't keep track."

"Garrett, it's been years since I saw you. How are you doing?" William said as he held out his hand toward the younger West.

"Good. It has been a while indeed, sir," Garrett replied.

Although his eyes were looking at her father, Jules had

the feeling that he was talking to her. It annoyed her that just the sound of his voice sent a shiver of pleasure down Jules' spine, and it took everything in her not to show it. Too bad for her, his time away hadn't been long enough.

As if he'd heard her thoughts, Garrett turned to Jules, and she could see the smile fighting to show up on his lips. He'd left town years ago, and she was destroyed, but in the back of her mind, Jules knew there was a chance he'd returned. After all, his family was still in the area. It didn't help that their parents were good friends. She was also still close with his twin sisters, Allie and Lily, even if her friendship with him had crashed and burned, and his older brother was engaged to one of her best friends. What she hadn't been expecting was for him to show up out of the blue with Rae and Flint at the Green Hat several weeks ago.

Afterwards, she'd asked the twins if they'd known he was coming back to town, and they'd both claimed they were as in the dark as she was. It seemed odd to her that Flint's younger brother would appear out of nowhere, without warning. It almost made her wonder if it was a coincidence that he was here tonight. Almost.

"It's been a long time, Jules."

His voice brought her out of her thoughts. His words, which were as smooth as honey due to his slight southern accent, slid over her and she had to fight from getting sucked in by his tone. She didn't want to like the sound of his voice. No, she preferred to hate it along with him. They were in polite company, and she couldn't ignore him, but that didn't mean she had to keep the bite from her tone. "Sure has. And it's Juliana now."

She could see that he was connecting the dots about her

comments in his mind as she watched her father raise an eyebrow at her out of the corner of her eye. Most people she was close to called her Jules, but she didn't want him to have that familiarity with her name or anything to do with her at all.

Terry coughed, cleared his throat and brought the attention back to him. "William, we need to catch up sometime soon. Golf? Maybe at the country club?"

"Sounds like a plan. Send me an email or have your assistant call mine."

Terry nodded. "It was nice seeing you both."

Jules gave him a big smile and could feel Garrett's gaze burning straight through her, leaving her feeling vulnerable in front of the men standing before her. But there was no way she would let him know. He wouldn't get that satisfaction from her.

Garrett didn't say another word as he followed Terry away. She was surprised he left without much of a fight.

"What was that all about, Jules?"

Her father's emphasis on her name told her he'd noticed her behavior just mere seconds ago.

"Nothing, Dad. Absolutely nothing."

2

"I'm sure the tablecloths that you picked out will be great." Jules tapped her pen on her desk, hoping at some point this exchange would be over. One of the reasons she was still in the office at this time of night was due to this call. "Is there anything else that you need for me tonight?"

"No. That will be all."

Under her breath, Jules almost said 'thank goodness.' Instead, she told the man on the other end to have a good night before she hung up the phone.

Wondering if she would make it to the night of the gala unscathed, Jules sighed, closing her eyes for a break from the glare of the computer screen. The Cartwright Foundation Gala was their biggest fundraising event of the year, and she was working overtime to ensure its success. Important names in the political and entertainment sphere would be attending, so there was no room for error. Typically, Jules' work involved writing press releases and making statements on behalf of the foundation. Now she was acting as an event planner. She probably should ask Liv for tips on dealing with the stress that came from putting together events like this. After all, she planned weddings for a living.

Suddenly, Jules heard a loud noise that came from the hallway. She hesitated, debating what she should do next. The noise erupted again. Someone wasn't happy. Chances were Jules was one of the few employees still left in the building, so where was the yelling coming from? She stood up from her desk, grabbed her phone, and crept across the room. The fact that she was hearing it through her closed door was shocking. After momentarily wondering if she should call security, Jules carefully inched open the door. It only took a split second for her to realize the shouting was coming from her father's office down the hall. As she made her way along the corridor, it didn't take long for her to understand the person who was yelling was on the phone because it was on speaker. That gave her a small sense of relief. At least she didn't have to deal with an angry person face-to-face.

When Jules reached her father's office, she heard a decisively slamming of the receiver, but she didn't think it had come from her father. She waited a few seconds before she knocked lightly and then she opened the door.

"Dad, is everything okay?" She gently closed the door, brow furrowing at the sight of her father with his head in his hands.

"Hi, sweetheart. Everything is fine. Is there anything you need?" He lifted his eyes to her, and she noticed the tension behind them. Although he said nothing was wrong, she knew something was troubling him, whether he wanted to admit it or not.

"No, I was just coming in to check on you. I heard a lot of yelling."

"It was nothing. What are you still doing here anyway? It's way past time for you to go home."

Jules was no fool, and she noticed he deflected her line of questioning. "I was wrapping up a few things before I headed out. Are you sure you don't need anything?"

"I'm sure." William stood up from his massive desk and walked toward his daughter. She stepped into her father's embrace, and visions of how he used to do this when she was younger flashed through her mind. Now she felt like the roles were reversed.

"Tell Mom I said hello."

He placed a quick kiss on her head. "Will do. Don't forget she wants you to come over for dinner this weekend."

"I know, and I'll be there. See you then."

Jules stepped back and smiled before turning around and walking out of her dad's office and back to her own. She flipped her blonde hair over one shoulder and grabbed her jacket and purse before closing her work laptop. She checked her phone and saw a message from Rae.

Rae: Hey, could you stop by my house on your way home from work? If you're busy, we can chat over the phone.

Jules: I don't have any fundraisers tonight, so I'm happy to stop by.

Part of her just wanted to head straight home, since it was after the time she was supposed to be working anyway, but if it was for a brief moment, she didn't really mind. Jules' office and apartment were less than a ten-minute drive from Rae and Flint's new home. She hit the light switch and headed toward the elevators. Once she was down in the lobby, she walked to her car and pulled out of the parking space, starting on the short journey to Rae's new home.

The light blue home with the soon-to-be-planted flower beds in front was absolutely perfect for her friend, and she couldn't be happier for all of the good fortune that she was having. When she was pulling up to the curb just before the driveway began, Rae opened the front door.

"Hey, I'm so sorry I invited you over on such short notice. I have wine if that is any consolation."

"It's not a problem, and I'm always down for some wine."

"Down? Stop hanging around Liv, okay?" Rae said with a laugh, backing up to let Jules pass her.

"So, what's up?" Jules said, taking her jacket off and giving it to Rae, who was waiting for it. "Every time I come over here, it looks even more beautiful."

"Thanks! It's coming together." Rae and Flint had been in their new place for a few months, and Rae still claimed they were slowly making the place homier—between Flint's busy congressional schedule and Rae's work schedule.

"Is Flint home?" Jules intentionally didn't mention the other person she knew was staying with them, because she couldn't stand him.

"He's not, and neither is Garrett." Rae looked at her, raising her eyebrow before going to retrieve the wine. Rae had mentioned Garrett had been staying with them for the last couple of weeks because he was waiting on his apartment to be ready.

"I didn't mention him on purpose."

"I know you didn't, but I was teasing you. Anyway, I invited you over because I missed you and wanted to hang out. Also, I was wondering if there might be a possibility for the Cartwright Foundation to team up with Wild Parks, Wild Lands to put together a gala to support environmental initiatives."

Jules took a sip of her wine; the liquid felt delicious going down her throat. "I have little control over that because I'm on the communications team, but I can let my dad know to see if he would be game for it. What did you have in mind? I'd probably have to talk to someone else on staff to handle the grant and do the paperwork, but I'm curious about what you were thinking."

"Great! I was hoping that we could brainstorm some ideas for what we could do? I'm hoping to do something different than your normal dinner fundraiser, but maybe involve educating children about the beauty of our environment and our public lands and that could encourage them to get out and explore it?"

Jules rolled the idea around her head as she took a sip of the wine in front of her. "I love that idea. It would be doing something for the community, and it would be way better than those stuffy dinners I have to go to all the time."

Rae chuckled. "Tell me how you really feel. Do you think it's something we could pull together relatively soon? I'm hoping we can do it before it gets too cold."

"If we could get everything approved, I don't see why planning couldn't start almost immediately." Another sip of wine made its way down her throat.

"Excellent! I can already see a potential event playing out in my head but, enough work talk; let's talk about some gossip. What the heck is up with you and Garrett?"

"Honey, I'm home!"

Rae laughed when she heard her fiancé come in the door.

She jumped up and ran over to Flint, laying a kiss on his lips. Jules rolled her eyes at the person behind them. With a smirk, Garrett took off his suit jacket without taking his eyes off of Jules.

"Of course, you'd be here."

"I'm staying here, so none of that is surprising. You, on the other hand, I didn't expect."

That makes two of us.

"Well, since the both of you are here, let's hash this out."

Garrett raised an eyebrow at Rae before Jules asked, "Hash this out?"

Rae gave Garrett a pointed look. "There's clearly something going on between the two of you, and if Garrett is going to be here on a more permanent basis, I just hope that you guys can get along because I don't want anyone to feel awkward around anyone else."

"I don't feel awkward at all."

Jules rolled her eyes at Garret's flippant response. "I can keep a cordial relationship with him. Just don't expect us to be best friends."

"Okay. I'll leave it at that..."

"Thank you." She wanted to add that Garrett knew what he did, but she stopped herself. Dealing with that would cause more drama, and that's the last thing she wanted right now.

Flint cleared his throat and said, "Jules, will you be staying for dinner? I can order something quickly so you can—"

Jules smiled. "No. That's alright. I have food at home. In fact, I should probably head out. I just came over to see what

Rae wanted to chat about the Cartwright Foundation giving a grant to Wild Parks, Wild Lands."

"Okay, I'll walk you to the door."

Jules could feel Garrett's gaze once again burning a hole through her as she stood up and prepared to go home. Once the two women were at Rae's front door, she turned to Jules and whispered, "Are you going to tell me what happened between you and Garrett?"

Jules shrugged. "Maybe someday, but I can't do it tonight. Having him reappear in my life has...been a lot, and I need time to process it all."

Rae nodded. "Okay, well, you know I'm here for you whenever you need it. Are you going to come to Green Hat on Friday?"

"Wouldn't miss it."

"I'll see you soon. Text me when you get home."

"Sure. Have a good night."

With that, Jules left Rae and Flint's home and drove back to her apartment. As soon as she opened her door and crossed over the threshold, some of the tension that had been living in her shoulders fled her body. Having Garrett appear not once, not twice, but three times unexpectedly in recent weeks did nothing to lower her stress levels.

When Jules entered her home, she couldn't help but smile. She'd spent so much time putting it together to fit her style and took great pride in showing it off. White and blush were the colors that were featured throughout her paint and decor choices and created her perfect private oasis. She'd taken her time picking out the pieces that were in her home, wanting to find ones that meant more to her versus buying things just because. Jules immediately felt the tranquil vibe that she'd instilled in her apartment as some of the stress began to leave her body. She tossed her keys on a tiny tray that she kept on the small table near the door

Sliding off her flats, Jules released her hair from the ponytail she'd thrown it up in hours ago and then sat down on her couch. The breath she'd been holding rushed out of her body. Jules was annoyed she was letting Garrett get to her. She'd told herself he wouldn't get to her anymore, but that was a lie given her reaction to just being in the same room as him. She took pride in remaining calm on the outside in stressful situations, yet here she was stewing over him when she should have been preparing for a relaxing evening. The thought irritated her further, and she turned on the television to take her mind off of him. She headed into the kitchen to heat up some leftovers from the evening before and yanked thoughts of Garrett and his sinful voice from her mind.

3

"Honey, I'm so glad you could make it tonight."

"Wouldn't miss it." Jules gave her mother a heartwarming smile as she took another bite of the lobster that Patricia, the Cartwrights' private chef, had prepared.

She tried to make it home as often as she could to spend time with her mother, Carol. Due to her father's somewhat hectic schedule, the times she spent with him were often at the office so having them both here was proving to be a treat.

Jules put the last forkful of her food in her mouth before gently placing the utensil down. "I'm stuffed. Everything was great."

"I concur. We'll have to tell Patricia when we see her next," William said, just before his phone rang. He glanced at the screen before turning to his wife. "I have to take this."

Carol sighed. "I thought we talked about you turning your phone on silent while we ate dinner?"

"I know, dear, but I've been waiting for this call. I'll be back as soon as I can." He took his napkin, loosely folded it, and placed it to the left of his plate. Walking to his wife, he placed a small kiss on the top of her hair. William then gave his daughter a small smile before he exited the dining room.

Carol smiled at her daughter. "I'm happy that I get to see you as often as I do. Your brother rarely comes home."

Jules had heard this argument a thousand times before. "Mom, you know it's hard for Sebastian to get back home. It makes sense that I would be home more frequently than he would."

Sebastian was her older brother who'd taken a job in Silicon Valley and never looked back. Between traveling the world and working on the West Coast, he didn't make it back to the D.C. area as often as their mother preferred.

"I know. I know. Doesn't mean I don't miss him."

Although Jules had never been in this situation where a mother missed their child, part of her could feel the tension rising whenever her brother was brought up. It was more often than not that this was brought up in her presence. The words got old after a while.

Jules steeled her spine before she said, "I'm sure he'll be coming for a visit soon." She made a mental note to herself that she would text him to see about it.

Her mother gave her a small smile. "I know you're right. Anyway, tell me about what's new in your life."

"You basically know everything."

"You didn't tell me you ran into Garrett recently."

"This is not the conversation I want to have, Mom."

"I know how hurt you were when he left, and how much that affected your—"

"I'm fine. Everything is fine. College was a long time ago, and I've moved on with my life." What she said was only partly true. Yes, Jules had put thoughts of Garrett on the back burner, but had she ever tried to forget him? No, and she wished she could. It didn't help that she was linked to the West family through a vast number of connections so escaping him would be a moot feat.

"Do you think you'll ever speak to him about what happened?"

Jules leaned back in the chair and shrugged, the facade of perfection she'd created over the years fading slightly. "I don't know, if I'm being honest."

Carol leaned forward, almost putting her elbows on the table before she placed her hands in her lap. "It might help you move on from the hurt and pain you feel."

"I'm not in pain anymore—"

"Sweetie, you don't need to sell me that story. I can see it in your eyes."

Although Jules wanted to fight her claim, she knew her mother was right. "I don't know, maybe I will. I just don't want to right now. I hadn't thought about any of it in such a long time and now the surge of emotions about it feels strange."

"Understandable. I'm just telling you, so you'll explore your options. You never know what you'll find out once you talk to him." Carol cleared her throat. "Do you want anything for dessert? Or a cup of coffee?"

"Mom, what do you know that I don't?"

"Nothing."

Carol's expression didn't give away that she knew anything, other than what she was telling Jules, so she took her mother at her word. She was grateful her mom had backed off the subject, although it hadn't left her mind.

"Yes, a cup of coffee sounds great."

WHEN JULES GOT HOME from dinner with her parents, the first thing she wanted to do was collapse on her couch. She loved spending time with her parents, but sometimes going home was strange for her. But being in the apartment where she had full control made all the difference in her life.

Instead, she tossed her keys on the small table near the door. She also laid the mail she'd picked up from the mailbox in the lobby and her purse on the table before she took off her red peacoat and removed her shoes. It had been a little chilly tonight so the heavier outwear was warranted.

When she turned around after putting her coat in the closet, she'd found that some of her mail had slipped off the table and landed on the floor. She hurried over to pick them up, leading to her rifling through the pieces of paper in her hand. Most of the mail was junk, and as she walked into her kitchen, she almost tossed everything into the recycling bin when she came across a light pink envelope that stopped her.

Her full name was printed across the front and nothing on the envelope showed any hints of who might be the sender. Thinking she had nothing to lose, Jules tossed the other mail in the bin and opened the envelope which had piqued her curiosity.

Jules withdrew what looked to be a children's card. The bright pink and purple design had 'Happy Birthday' written across the top in big bold letters. Curiosity got the best of her again because she opened the card, and the card began to sing 'Happy Birthday' to her.

"What in the world?" Jules couldn't deny that she was creeped out by the whole thing. It was a combination of the card itself, no return address, and the song playing from the card sounded like a dying toy. The card wasn't signed either.

She snapped the card shut and put it on her countertop. Who would send something like this? She walked back to the small table and grabbed her purse. Jules pulled out her phone and typed out a text before sending it to her group chat.

Jules: Who sent me the birthday card?

She stared at her phone, willing one of her friends to respond to her message, but of course, no one did. In a huff, she walked back into the kitchen and examined the card again. Coming up empty handed once more, Jules placed it back on the counter and snapped a few pictures with her phone. She sent the images to the chat, hoping that would spur a response because she was impatiently waiting to hear back and get to the bottom of who sent it. She sighed when she got a reply.

Eve: Nah. It's not even your birthday.

Rae: No. Never saw that before.

And it didn't take long for Liv to reply and for Eve to add to hers.

Liv: Although I think it would be worth a laugh, nope over here as well.

Eve: Is this a trick question?

There was also that point as well. Her birthday was a ways away, so why would anyone want to send her a birthday card now, let alone one meant for a child? If she had to be honest, the more she thought about it, the more creeped out she was by the entire thing.

"Who sent this?" she asked herself as she turned the card

over in her hand once more. "Who would think this is funny?"

After staring at it for a second more, Jules put the card down on the counter and walked over to sit on her white couch. There was no way she was spending more time thinking about this prank than necessary. She leaned over and pulled out her planner, deciding to take some time to write out her schedule and a to-do list for the next few days while she was in the mood to do so.

But every so often, Jules would look over at her kitchen, where she could barely see the card, wondering if there was more to the birthday card than met the eye.

4

"Hi, Dad," Jules answered her desk phone. She found it a bit odd he was calling her instead of just walking down the hall but shook it off.

"Hey! Do you have time for a quick meeting with Terry West?"

Her eyes bugged out of her head for a moment. She was thankful that he hadn't been standing in front of her when he made the announcement. Jules looked at her calendar to see if anyone had told her this meeting would be occurring. "Nothing is preventing me from going, but I thought you guys were going to meet one-on-one? Something about golf being involved?"

She vaguely remembered the short conversation that they had had at the fundraiser. Most of the oxygen in the room had been taken up by the fact she and Garrett were, once again, in each other's presence so she hadn't been paying as close attention as she should have been.

"It was, but he brought Garrett with him, and I thought you might want to sit in on the conversation. You talked about wanting to be included in more high-level meetings, so I thought this might be the perfect opportunity."

Of course, her ambition to succeed at work and eventually be president of the foundation one day wouldn't let her talk her way out of this. Plus, there was a small part of her that was curious about what the conversation would be about anyway. "I'll be in there in a couple of minutes."

"Sounds good."

Jules groaned. She usually was able to adapt to a changing situation on a dime but having to face Garrett multiple times on such short notice was enough to send her mind spiraling. She was just getting used to him being in the same city as her, and now it seemed that every time she looked around, he was there. Well, at least with their fathers in the room, surely the conversation would stick to business. Or so she hoped.

Jules stood up, put on the navy blazer that she'd worn to work over the white sheath dress, and pulled out her phone. She checked her appearance and thought that the light makeup she'd put on this morning was still holding up well. Her hand pulled on the messy ponytail she'd thrown her hair in because she didn't think she had any in-person meetings today, letting her hair fall around her shoulders. With a sigh, she headed down the hallway to her father's office. Taking a deep breath before she knocked on the door, Jules waited for him to announce that she could come in.

When he did, she opened the door and the first thing she saw was her father greeting her with a giant grin. "There she is. Welcome, Jules. Let me just grab this chair for you."

"Thanks, Dad," she said as she closed the door behind her.

When she turned back around, her father was pulling another chair up to the small conference table in his office, and she found Terry and Garrett West both now standing to greet her. Terry smiled at her and shook her hand. Although they were still in a formal setting, his demeanor was warmer than it had been the night of the fundraiser they had attended. That made sense given the change of location and the more secluded space. After all, she had spent a lot of time at his home when she was growing up.

Jules held her breath as she turned to Garrett once she was done shaking his father's hand. Garrett's expression differed from both of the other men, and she felt her pulse jump when he held out his hand to shake hers. The grip that his hand held on hers was firm yet warm and made her thoughts run wild. She couldn't read his face, something she'd been able to do quite easily when they were younger. Jules didn't know if that was a result of being apart for so many years or if something had changed him.

That was definitely not the only thing that changed. Garrett West had always been handsome, but even with his body covered by the suit, she could see that he'd grown more muscular over the years. Standing closer to him now than she had been at any point over the last few times they'd bumped into each other confirmed every notion that had run through her head when she saw him. His broad chest and muscular biceps exhibited power, and she didn't think she knew of many people who would want to be in his way if he wanted to get to something.

Because the black suit fit him perfectly, it wasn't hard for her to see that his legs matched his upper body and that he clearly did what it took to stay in shape. Jules made sure not to check him out for too long because she didn't want things to get awkward and wanted to maintain a show of professionalism. Just because she didn't particularly like him, didn't mean that she couldn't silently admire his body.

It seemed as if her admiration wasn't so quiet after all because she could see the sparkle in his eye when her eyes made their way back up to his. It was clear that she'd gotten caught checking him out. She shrugged it off because she felt the heat of his gaze when she entered the room and knew that her years of taking barre classes and cardio had been excellent for her body, and it showed.

"Nice to see you again, Juliana."

The way her full first name rolled off his tongue almost made her quiver, but she held strong. Her body was determined to betray her, but she wouldn't let it happen. The mask she'd worked so hard to put in place was firmly back on and just because he was here, she was determined to not have it removed.

"Likewise." The words fell smoothly off her tongue, and she kept her tone even. No one in the room would know that she didn't actually mean it.

William clapped his hands together once. "Well, let's begin."

Everyone sat down in the chairs around a table that William had installed in his office, and Jules opened her notebook, ready to write anything down that seemed relevant to her.

"The reason why Terry and I wanted to get together to have this meeting is because both he and Gladys want to join together with me and Carol and put together scholarships that pay for several high school seniors from underserved communities to go to college. All expenses paid. This was an idea that both Gladys and Carol had and mentioned it in passing, and we want to make this happen."

Jules looked at her father wide-eyed and she could see out of the corner of her eye that Garrett adjusted his posture. This was a surprise to him as well.

"Well, I, for one, think that this is a great idea. If you've already been working on this behind the scenes, I think it would be a great idea to announce this at the Cartwright Foundation Gala."

William smiled at his only daughter. "We are on the same wavelength."

The conversation continued between the group, and Jules noted that while Garrett did speak every so often and did seem attentive, he didn't add much to the conversation. That was probably more due to him not really being involved in charity work or working with a foundation.

"This all sounds like a splendid idea. I'll figure out where everything stands and see if we can pull this off to make an announcement at the gala."

As William and Terry beamed at her, Garrett cleared his throat and said, "I'm a little lost with everything, but I'd love to help. Juliana, maybe we could have another meeting over dinner, and you can tell me more about all of this work and where I would fit in?"

"That would be a good idea since you have some down time right now at your job." William looked at Garrett before looking back at his daughter. "This is all up to you, though, sweetheart. I don't know your schedule or how busy you are."

Jules was annoyed that Garrett had put her on the spot in

front of their fathers. "I'll have to check my schedule, but I'll get back to you."

She had no intention of getting back to him if she could help it, because she knew this was a way to trap her into going to dinner with him. This time she had no problem reading the expression on his face, and she knew he'd stop at nothing to get his way.

5

The next week flew by in a blur. Jules couldn't complain because things were relatively quiet for her. She was so happy that it was now Friday morning, and she was so close to enjoying what she hoped to be a quiet weekend. As she stretched her neck due to some soreness she had endured due to the barre class she had taken the evening before, her phone buzzed, drawing her attention away from the press release she was reading over.

Liv: So, what's this about you running into Flint's younger brother and sparks flying? Did you get any of that aggression out? ;)

The winky face that was included with the text message made Jules groan loudly.

Jules: I hope you mean angry sparks because that's the only thing going on here.

Liv: Rae told me about what happened at her place. Apparently, he couldn't take his eyes off of you until you left and started quizzing Rae.

Of course, Liv would have taken that as meaning she

wanted to bang him. His asking questions about her should have shown that this was all one-sided, but given that Liv wasn't there to see it in person, she couldn't blame her. Also, Rae hadn't mentioned him talking about her after she'd left.

Jules: What did Rae say happened after I left?

Liv: I knew you would be interested in that.

Jules closed her eyes and let out a deep breath. She couldn't say she was surprised by Liv's antics, but she was annoyed with having to deal with it.

Jules: Liv…

Liv: I don't know if I've ever seen you annoyed before…anyway he was essentially trying to catch up on your life. What you were doing. Things like that. Nothing invasive.

Wouldn't it have been easier to ask his twin sisters? Then again, they might have actually given him shit for it.

Liv: Is everything okay?

Jules: Yes. Garrett is just a sore subject. Don't worry about him.

Liv: You telling me not to worry about it makes it seem like I should.

Jules rolled her eyes. Of course, Liv would pick up on that.

Jules: He asked me out to dinner. To talk about the foundation and a scholarship that we are helping our parents with.

Liv: What's wrong with that?

Jules: Nothing except for I think he's trying to use it as an excuse to talk to me about other things…like about us.

Liv: Maybe it's time for you to talk about those things? Based on what you said, it's been years so it could be time to hash it out.

Jules: Now you sound like Eve. I need to get a couple of things done so I might be a little delayed in responding.

Liv: No worries. I guess I have brides I should respond to…so I can keep my job. Talk to you later.

Jules chuckled and shook her head as she placed her phone back down on her desk and tried to focus her attention back on the press release. When her phone buzzed again, Jules bit back a sigh.

Garrett: *Hey this is Garrett. Wasn't sure if you still had my number. Anyway, I still wanted to take you out to dinner.*

Her heart skipped a beat as she read his message over and over again. Part of her wanted to accept his invitation, but the logical part of her brain told her she didn't need this complication right now.

Jules: *Look Garrett, I don't think I can. Super busy with work at the moment. To be honest, I forgot you even mentioned this.*

Jules couldn't deny that she felt pretty good about pointing it out. When she went with someone, whether it was on a personal or professional level, she usually tried to confirm a time and day pretty quickly. She had to admit, she preferred that because it made her think that they thought that her time was valuable. Not that she had any expectations about whatever he was trying to pull.

Garrett: *Is this your way of blowing me off? ;-)*

The winky face he included at the end was endearing and almost made her wonder if he and Liv were talking behind her back. Either way, it still didn't sway her. There was still a lot of history there that she didn't want to dig up now, if ever. The past needed to stay there for her sanity.

Jules: *No. Our foundation's big gala is coming up soon and I'm helping out with it. Maybe we can arrange for a quick meeting in the office?*

She hated that she felt the need to explain why she couldn't do something, but she typed out the excuse and pressed send before she could think to stop herself. Her phone buzzed almost immediately.

Garrett: *Okay if that works for you. Let me know if your evening plans change. I would still like to take you out to dinner even if it's for old time's sake.*

Her mind wanted to dig deeper into what this could mean, but that was put on pause when a knock on her office door distracted her from the text messages. It looked like she wasn't going to get any work done today if this kept up.

"Come in," she said as she pushed her office chair back, ready to greet whomever was standing on the other side.

Normally, when her father came into her office, she'd smile at him, but this time, a look of concern crossed her face as she quickly walked over to him.

The first thing she noticed was the paleness of her father's skin. The normal brightness that shone in his eyes was dimmed.

"Is everything all right?" The question sounded foolish, even to her ears. It was clear something was wrong.

"I'm fine. I'm just a little winded."

"Come here and sit down." Jules guided him over to a chair in front of her desk and then sat down in the one opposite his. "Do I need to call an ambulance?"

"No, no, no." William took a deep breath. "I think I was moving faster than I should've been. I actually came down here to check on you."

Jules appreciated her father's concern about her, but his statement was odd. What was he getting at? "Dad, should something have happened to me?"

William shook his head. "No, but I need you to promise me this."

"What? What is it that you want me to promise you?"

"If you see something strange, you'll tell me immediately."

If William was trying to soothe her anxiety, he failed completely. "I don't know what you're—"

"Promise. Me. This."

His stern emphasis told her there was no negotiating the matter. The seriousness of his demeanor and the harshness of his tone made her nerves jump. She couldn't remember a time he'd talked to her this way. It was enough to get him the answer he desired.

"Yes. I promise."

That seemed to be enough to ease the tension that built in the room as soon as he'd entered. William gave his daughter a small smile and patted her on the hand.

"Do you want me to drive you home?"

"I have meetings to attend and a few calls to make. I'm feeling better now that I've seen you. I love you, Jules."

The tone of his voice lost the edge it had had just moments before. What replaced it was worry, and his refusal to discuss it with her made the situation that much worse.

"I love you too."

William rubbed his hands down his pant legs before he stood up. "Are you hanging out with your friends tonight?"

"That's the plan, unless you need me for something."

William gave her a half smile. "No. On second thought, maybe I'm going to see if your mother wants to go out to dinner tonight. Just the two of us."

"That's a lovely idea. I'm sure she'd enjoy it."

"Yeah, we don't do that as much as we should... I'll see you later, sweetheart."

"Bye, Dad." Jules watched as her father left the office as quickly as he came in and wondered what the hell was going on.

THE REST of the day was uneventful, and soon Jules found herself grabbing her blazer off the back of her chair as she prepped to head out for the evening. Instead of wearing her peacoat tonight, she opted to go out in just the blazer, hoping it wouldn't be too chill. At least the humidity that the D.C. area was known for during the summer and early fall was gone. She couldn't wait to sit down at the Green Hat and let the stress of the workday leave her mind. It felt as if it had been too long since they'd last gotten together, and she couldn't wait to have that rectified tonight.

Jules pulled her long blonde hair out from her collar before she walked out of her office. She ended up wandering down the hall to see if her father was still there. She smiled when she found his office dark and empty; it seemed as if he'd taken his own advice to spend some time with her mother that evening. With that, she turned around and walked toward the elevators that would lead her to the outside world and to happy hour with her friends.

"You don't know how much I needed this." Liv took another sip of the drink in her hand.

Without missing a beat, Eve said, "By the long sip of that rum and coke you just took, we can all see that."

Jules chuckled at Liv and Eve's banter. Although she wouldn't say it out loud, she agreed with Liv. She needed this moment to unwind with her friends. "Is Rae ever going to get here?"

Eve cut her eyes to Jules. "Now you know the answer to that question."

Jules shrugged and took a sip of her wine. It wasn't shocking that Rae was late, and her tardiness had become a running joke within their circle.

"Maybe Flint is showing her how to follow his yellow brick road?"

Jules choked on her wine and stared at Liv in amazement. Why she chose to drink or eat around Liv at this point was beyond her.

"I heard that."

As Jules was wiping her mouth, she looked over and found Rae standing near their table with her arms folded and a smirk on her face. Clearly, she hadn't taken offense to what Liv had said.

Before anyone could say something else, Rae continued, "I was at work, thank you very much."

Liv wasn't about to let this go. "When has that stopped you?"

Eve chimed in. "She has a point and—"

"Enough both of you. Are you sure you didn't start drinking before you came here? I'm not that late."

Rae's pointed stare at Liv caused Jules to bite back the laughter threatening to fall from her mouth as Rae sat in the empty seat across from her. Communicating with her friends over texts or video chats didn't do any of their in-person time together justice.

As if he knew that Rae had just arrived, John, the owner of the Green Hat, walked over to their table with a big smile.

"Good evening. It's been a little while."

Jules nodded with a grin on her face. "It has been too long for my liking."

John smiled at her before turning to Rae to take her order. When he left to go get her drink, the women focused on each other.

"Liv, I'm surprised you were able to make it this evening. You mentioned you might have had a conflict."

"Yeah...that 'conflict' was cancelled."

Jules was expecting her to say it was something related to work given it was early fall once again, and many weddings were taking place now.

"This sounds like it wasn't wedding planning related," Eve added, before taking a drink from her glass.

"I don't even want to talk about it."

That was unlike Liv, not wanting to share the recent events that had happened in her life. Jules patted her hand and gave her a reassuring smile before turning to Rae. "Speaking of weddings, Rae, have you done any wedding planning?"

Rae scoffed and gave John a smile when he placed a glass of wine in front of her. "Thanks, John." She then turned back to her friends as John walked away. "I haven't done much of anything wedding related, and don't feel a burning desire to do so."

Eve turned to her. "Cold feet?"

"In terms of marrying Flint? No. Not at all. It's the wedding planning part that has me stressed out."

"Hi. I'm a wedding planner."

The table chuckled at Liv's admission before turning to Rae again. "I don't want you to have to work on my wedding day. Honestly, it's the hoopla around trying to plan a wedding to someone...with his background."

Jules could understand that completely. Getting married to someone who was famous due to politics, among other things, and given his and his family's connections throughout the area, it would be a huge amount of pressure on anyone. Hell, she felt similarly to anyone who she might marry down the line.

"Why not just elope?"

"I can't say I haven't thought about it. We might end up doing it if I get fed up enough. Potentially going to piss off a lot of people, but you can't please everyone so..."

"You could also just have two separate events. Something small for family and friends and maybe a bigger reception for associates that would be expected to be invited to Flint West's wedding?" Liv took a sip after throwing her suggestion out there.

"That is an idea..." Rae's eyes shifted toward Jules. "Did you ever find out who sent you that birthday card?"

Jules shook her head. "No one that I contacted said they had. I would think that it was sent to me by mistake, but my name was written on the envelope. I asked my building's security if they noticed anything, since the card didn't have a stamp on it and I assumed someone dropped it off. Nothing there either."

She could say that she had put the whole incident out of her mind and hadn't thought about the card since she received it, but that would be a lie. It popped up every time she walked into her kitchen and found the envelope sitting there, almost taunting her with its presence.

"Listen, I wonder if—"

Rae stopped speaking, and her mouth dropped open. As her eyes widened, Jules turned to look in the direction that Rae was staring in. Her expression soon mirrored Rae's as she found Garrett storming toward their table.

When he reached where they were sitting, his eyes were staring straight at Jules and the first words out of his mouth were, "You're coming with me."

"No, I'm not." Jules could have growled at the man in front of her.

"Jules, this isn't the time to fight me on this."

"Don't call me Jules. You don't get to come in here and tell me what to do."

"Juliana, let's go."

The strong emphasis on her name almost made her tremble, but she wasn't sure if it was due to anger or arousal. It wasn't enough to make her forget what he was saying to her right now. Although she could feel the embarrassment floating through her body, all decorum flew out the window. "No. Fuck you."

As the harshly whispered words left her lips, the other women at the table gasped. Jules was pretty sure they'd never heard her curse before. Well, there was a first time for everything. Jules took a second to look around to see if anyone at the surrounding tables had heard the argument, but it seemed as if no one had.

"Don't make me drag you out of here."

Garrett's words drew her gaze back to him, and she glared. "You wouldn't dare. There are plenty of witnesses around, including my friends."

Garrett took a deep breath. It wouldn't take a genius to find out he was trying to calm himself down. "For your own safety, you need to come with me. And I'm sure you don't want to cause a scene."

Safety? What was going on? She also couldn't deny that he had her there. She lived her life intentionally trying to not cause any trouble and being what everyone would deem the perfect person.

Two phones buzzed on the table in rapid succession, but Jules didn't even bother looking to see whose phone it was. All that mattered was showing Garrett that he couldn't just storm and tell her what to do.

"Jules."

Jules' eyes flew over to look at Rae, wondering what she wanted.

"You should go with Garrett."

Out of the corner of her eye, she saw Eve nodded in agreement before looking back down at her phone.

Liv's eyes jumped between each person at the table. "What do you three know that the rest of us don't?"

"I'll explain to her in the car, and Kane and Flint should be on their way here at any moment. But, Juliana, you have to come with me now."

With a huff, Jules stood up and grabbed her purse. "Fine."

"Close out any tabs you all have," Garrett said as he tossed some bills on the table.

Jules summarized it was enough to cover their drinks, tip, tax and then some. Just as he turned to look at her, the door to the Green Hat opened and in walked Kane and Flint.

"Juliana, your friends are fine, come on now."

The seriousness in his voice scared her. She nodded, figuring if she wanted to argue with him more, she could do it on the way to wherever they were going. Once she walked past him, she felt Garrett's hand land on her lower back. Jules reached behind her and removed it. She didn't want him rocking her world any more than he just had, and she knew his touch would make her lose all control of her senses. Thankfully, any sort of feelings she'd had as a result of the wine were thrown out the window because Garrett barging in sobered her up quickly.

He held the door open for her, and once she was seated in the black SUV, he breathed a sigh of relief.

"What's going on? Where are we going?"

Garrett didn't say anything as he drove down the street.

She watched as his gaze bounced from looking through the windshield, to looking out the side and rearview mirrors.

"Garrett, I want to know what is going on. The only reason I'm here is because Rae and Eve said I should be. If they know what's going on, I deserve to know too. Especially if this has anything to do with me, which it seems as if it does."

"I'm making sure we aren't being followed."

Garrett's words caused her mood to shift from anger to fear. "Why should we be concerned about being followed?"

"Because your father was threatened, and told if he didn't do what they asked, you'd be killed."

7

"Come on...come on," Jules said as the line continued to ring.

Garrett's announcement stopped any further protests from Jules, but it forced her to fish her phone out to call her parents. When the call went to voicemail again, she hung up. Her hope had been to have one of them confirm what was going on, but that looked like it wouldn't be the case.

"Couldn't reach them?" Garrett asked when she took the phone away from her ear.

She opened and closed her mouth twice, but focused her attention on looking straight ahead, even as she tried to sort her racing thoughts out. A tear flowed down her cheek, one she quickly wiped away in hopes that Garrett wouldn't notice.

"Are my parents okay? Neither one of them are answering their phones."

"Yes, they're fine. We have people watching them, but we aren't as concerned about them, because you were the one mentioned in the letter."

"Someone sent them a letter? Threatening to kill me?"

Garrett nodded.

"What did the letter say? And where are we going?"

"Are you sure you want to know?"

Jules swallowed hard. "Yes. I want to know everything that you know."

"It was addressed to William and said if he didn't admit his past sins, his pride and joy would be taken from him. Inch by inch."

"That could be a number of things. Dad loves my mother, my brother and me, the foundation, golf—"

"What would hurt him the most, Juliana? Answer me honestly."

Jules' eyes darted around the vehicle, not wanting to admit what was on the tip of her tongue. "Probably either me, Sebastian, or my mother. We're the only family he has left alive."

"We're hedging our bets on you, and that's why we are in this SUV right now."

"Where are we going?"

"To one of Knox's safe houses for a couple of days."

"Wait, what!" Jules' words came out as almost a screech. "No, I'm going home."

"We're going to send a team to your apartment to make sure there isn't anything in it that could harm you, but it's going to take some time to get them in place."

"What? How dare you!" Rage burned through her at Garrett's admission. "And what the hell is Knox?"

"You've changed a lot since I left."

His statement took her back and quelled some of her anger. The way her emotions were flipping and all of the events from tonight, Jules knew there was no way she was walking out of this SUV without a headache.

"You mean I've grown up?"

"That too. But I never imagined you letting cuss words fly."

"I don't, but given the circumstances, I don't think you can blame me."

"Good point." Garrett glanced at her out of the corner of his eye. "You'll have everything you need at the safe house, so don't worry about anything back at your apartment."

His slight reminder about what was happening incited her anger once more. "I want to go home."

"It's not safe for you—"

"Take me to Virginia. What you are doing right now is holding me against my will."

The last word came out as almost a growl, and she could see her comment had upset him. The ticking of his jaw and the tightening of his hand on the steering wheel were easy signs her words had had their intended effect.

"Fine."

Garrett swung the car around and headed in the opposite direction. Jules sat quietly in the car, debating whether or not he was actually taking her home. If he wasn't heading toward Virginia, she would know soon enough. She couldn't deny she was somewhat shocked he had listened to her request. After all, he seemed pretty gung-ho about taking her to the safe house. A debate raging in her head amongst everything else was whether or not she needed to flee the car.

Part of her wanted to believe the then boy she had grown to trust was still inside of Garrett, but Jules didn't know what the man he had become was capable of. Their falling out also played a role in the battle currently raging in her mind.

When she started to see some familiar buildings, Jules began to relax. She was still on guard due to everything going on, but at least they were going in the right direction. Jules assumed Garrett wasn't trying to take a prisoner, and if he was, he had a horrible way of going about doing it. Outside of him leaving the Green Hat with her in front of a lot of witnesses, she still had her cell phone, purse, and coat. The doubts she'd had about his version of events faded slightly once she took a moment to consider more of the details that led up to her being in this SUV.

Jules took the phone out of her purse and checked her notifications. She wasn't surprised to see text messages flying back and forth in her best friends group chat.

Eve: Jules is everything alright? Where are you?

Rae: Has Garrett filled you in? Are you okay?

Liv: Why aren't you answering?

Jules: I'm fine. I just told Garrett to take me to my apartment. I think he's filled me in.

The fact she didn't know for sure or trust he had given her all of the information spoke volumes.

Liv: You think?

Eve: I'm not sure how safe that is given the threat given to your father. We don't want anything to happen to you.

Jules: I'll be fine, trust me.

Even though she was the one who typed the words out, Jules didn't know how much she trusted them herself.

Feeling overwhelmed from the messages being sent to her, Jules put her phone back into her purse and dropped it at her feet.

"Everything okay?" It was the first time she'd heard Garrett say anything in a bit.

"I think so," she whispered and looked out of the window. When he didn't say anything else, Jules didn't know if she'd hoped he would have or was happy to have the silence pass between the two of them.

When they crossed the bridge into Virginia, Jules turned to Garrett and asked, "Do you know where I live?"

Garrett nodded, not bothering to hide.

"How?"

"Outside of me figuring you lived pretty close to Rae and Flint enough to drop everything and head over there after work on short notice? Your father told me."

Jules closed her eyes, begging herself not to react to the news he'd just dropped. She took deep breaths, calming the annoyance she felt. The mask which had taken years for her to perfect slid onto her face, hiding the emotions that dared to be unleashed.

Jules took one final deep breath and opened her eyes, a neutral expression painted on her face. "So, he asked you to come save me."

"I guess you could say that. He knew I would do anything in my power to protect you."

"How would you know that? Since when do you and my father talk about things like that? It's also very convenient that I can't confirm any of this with my father or mother right now."

"Looks like you're going to have to trust me then."

Jules let his words hang in the air by not responding. There was no way she was going down this road again. She refused to let her emotions take over and decided to be more logical about the situation. It was then she realized she still didn't know what he'd meant by Knox.

"What is Knox?" she asked again.

Garrett glanced at her and sighed. "Knox is a security firm that works on cases for people who want protection or justice and have the money to pay for the services."

That struck a chord with Jules. Just how dangerous could this job be? "And you work for them?"

Garrett nodded.

"And things can be...unpredictable?"

Garrett studied her before turning his focus back to the road. "Unpredictable as in dangerous? Yes, it can."

Jules swallowed hard and wondered what made her father think Garrett was the best person to protect her, given the circumstances? She assumed that Knox more than likely employed plenty of people so why had he zeroed in on him? Surely it wasn't because Terry and he were friends, he wouldn't choose someone to guard her based on that, would he?

Rather than voice her opinion, Jules decided to stay quiet as Garrett drove them closer and closer to Arlington, Virginia.

"Okay, I need you directing from here. Was I right about you not living too far from Rae and Flint?"

Jules nodded. "You're going to need to make a left at this light and then keep going straight."

He followed the directions perfectly and pulled up in front of the luxury apartment she was renting. He parked the vehicle and opened up the driver side door.

"Where are you going?"

"To make sure you get to your apartment safely."

Jules glanced at him out of the side of her eye. "Garrett, I think I can go up to my apartment by myself."

"It doesn't mean you have to. I'm doing this so that when I tell your father you don't want my services, the least I can say is I made sure you made it into your apartment safely."

Jules exhaled loudly, figuring she wouldn't win this fight, and opened her door. The two walked through the lobby quickly, with Garrett tailing closely behind her. She couldn't deny having him near her did bring a sense of comfort, even though she wanted him to leave her alone.

The two rode up the elevator in silence, although Jules felt as if the sounds of her thoughts bouncing around in her brain were as loud as a rock concert. The elevator was taking its sweet time, or so it seemed. It could be because she was standing next to him, the man she longed to forget, despite the chances of that happening were nil.

When the elevator doors finally opened, a rush of air fled her lungs. Jules led the way to her apartment, and when she was in front of her door, she turned to face Garrett.

"Well, this is me," she said. That was her way of politely telling him he could leave now.

"I'm not leaving until you're on the other side of the door."

Jules stared at him for a second, before turning to open the door. When she tried to place her key in the top lock, the door gave way a little, showing that it wasn't closed. Garrett noticed it immediately and pulled Jules away from the entrance.

"You didn't leave your door open, did you?"

She could see him reaching for something near his pants

out of the corner of his eye, but her eyes were still fixated on her door being open.

"Of course not. Are the people you sent to my apartment here now?"

Garrett shook his head but said nothing. If she wasn't nervous about the situation, her tone would have been more sarcastic. Jules finally moved her eyes from the door and looked at him, noting the gun in his hand. Her eyes widened as she swallowed hard.

"I'm going to go in and check to make sure there's no one in there. I want you to stay out here."

"I want to go in there with you." There was no way she was staying out there where she could be considered a sitting duck, especially if someone had threatened to kill her.

Her thoughts must've made sense to Garrett because he nodded slightly and gestured for her to follow him. "When I open the door, I want you to turn on the closest light. I assume there is one near the door."

Jules nodded; afraid her voice would give away her nervousness.

He slowly pushed the door open, and Jules did as she was told. What greeted her was a sight she'd thought she would never see: her entire apartment ransacked.

Jules felt herself begin to shake as Garrett quickly made sure they were the only ones still in the apartment without trying to disturb the scene. He had holstered his gun by the time he reappeared in front of her and had his phone out.

"Garrett? I think I want to stay at the safe house tonight after all."

8

"Ms. Cartwright?"

Jules stopped walking toward the door and turned around. She could feel Garrett near her back, so she knew that he'd stopped walking too. The team that Garrett said would arrive had done so and her apartment was abuzz with activity. People were trying to find clues about who might have broken into her apartment.

"I'm sorry to keep you a little bit longer, but I have a couple more questions before you head out."

Jules looked back at Garrett who gave her a slight nod before he pulled his phone out. Once she answered the questions, she walked back over to Garrett who led her out to his vehicle.

Jules stared out of the SUV as the vehicle drove through the streets of Washington, D.C. Tears streamed down her face, and she did her best to hide them from the other occupant in the car. She quietly sniffled, hoping the slight noise wouldn't bring attention to her.

The ride from her apartment continued in silence. It was

about ninety minutes after she and Garrett had discovered the disaster zone that had been her apartment.

Chairs were overturned, lamps destroyed, papers tossed everywhere. The painstaking care she had taken in designing the apartment how she wanted it and making it into a home that she was proud of had been currently for naught. She wasn't sure who could have done such a thing nor was she sure of a motive because nothing she could see had been stolen. What she did know was that she couldn't stay there. Not tonight or potentially ever again.

There were a lot of people who needed to answer how this could've happened.

Instead of calling the police, Garrett had convinced her to let him call in his fellow coworkers from Knox. It would be the easiest way to keep this out of the news, and the people who worked with him were highly trained in areas such as this.

"You know, I wonder if this is how Flint felt when his campaign office was destroyed."

"I'm sure this feels much worse to you. That is your personal home, your sanctuary, and someone has violated it."

Garrett's words caused the tears to fall faster. There was no way she'd be able to hide how upset she was now. He reached over and placed his hand lightly on her knee, rubbing small circles on her leg. Although she couldn't feel the direct heat of his touch due to the slacks she was wearing, just having the weight of his hand on her was sending her emotions into overdrive. It was also providing a sense of security that she hadn't had since the moment she'd stepped into her place.

"There should be some tissues in the glove compartment."

Jules quickly reached over and unlocked the compartment and grabbed the tissues, wiping at the tears. "Did you suspect that something like this might happen? Is that why you suggested going to the safe house immediately after storming into the Green Hat?"

"No. Given the threat that was made to your father, I thought the best idea was to get you somewhere safe as quickly as possible. We probably would have known about your apartment in a few more hours anyway."

His statements made her raise an eyebrow. "Why would you have known about my apartment anyway?"

"Someone at Knox would have been watching it, no matter what. That is part of the reason why it was so easy to get them there to investigate more thoroughly. It helped that a team was already heading to your place to make sure that it was safe."

Jules didn't know how she felt about that, but at this point in time, there was no use in arguing. She wanted to do whatever she could to keep her and her family and friends safe, and if that meant dealing with all of this in this manner, then so be it. That was why she decided not to ask to stay with one of her friends.

"Have you heard from my father?"

"Didn't he or your mother reach out to you?"

Jules almost glared at him for answering her question with a question, but there were more important matters to deal with. "Can't you just give me a straight answer?"

Garrett glanced at her out of the corner of his eye. "I did update your father, because he is the one who hired me."

So, they did know. "And they're okay? I hope?" Jules hated that she was asking him for confirmation because she couldn't reach her parents. She'd tried calling them again when they got back in the SUV, but neither parent answered.

That was when Jules realized it had been a good while since she'd checked her phone due to everything that had occurred over the last few hours.

Her decision was further cemented when Garrett pulled into an underground garage. It didn't take long for the couple to take the bags that Jules had quickly packed out of the trunk. That's when she noticed Garrett pulled out another black duffel bag and dropped it at his feet.

"Oh, you already had a bag for yourself."

Garrett shrugged. "I usually keep it in the car, just in case I need it."

"That makes sense, given your line of work, which I don't know much about."

"I'll tell you what I can when we get upstairs."

Garrett grabbed most of their bags while Jules helped with one of the others and led her to a door. Once the door was open, she waltzed through and found herself in front of a set of elevators. It took a bit of maneuvering, but soon the two were headed up to the safe house that Jules hoped she would only stay at for the next couple of nights.

Jules didn't know what to expect when Garrett opened the door to the apartment, but it wasn't this. The apartment was a small step down from a penthouse suite and she could see that from just the small section she could see. The door opened up into a short hallway, and from there, she could see a living area that had a large couch and a big screen television. Although she couldn't tell from where she was, she assumed that there were some expensive electronics sitting in the tv stand.

"There is one bedroom, straight down that hallway that is all yours."

Jules nodded but had conflicting thoughts flying through her mind. "Where will you be staying?"

"I'll be sleeping on the couch."

Guilt rose in Jules' stomach. The couch was of nice quality, and the reason he was sleeping on it was due to someone threatening her life. Given his tall, muscular body and the size of that couch, she knew it wouldn't be comfortable.

"Look, I'm smaller and could easily fit on the couch. Why don't you sleep in the bedroom where I'm sure the bed will have a lot more room?"

"No. I want you to have the bedroom."

"But I'm fine taking the couch–"

"You're sleeping in that bedroom. End of discussion."

With that, Garrett took her bags and started walking down the hallway.

"Do you always get your way?"

Garrett looked over his shoulder, a smirk growing on his face. "Yes, and it is about time you started to figure that out." He continued on his way to the bedroom.

Jules sighed as she moved into the kitchen that she spotted when they entered the apartment. She wanted to avoid running into Garrett while he put her bags down, but once he was done, she was going to call her parents to fill them in on what Garrett hadn't. When had he even notified them? When another member of team Knox questioned her after they'd showed up at the apartment?

Her first thought was to check if there was any bottled

water in the fridge, and if there wasn't, she'd hunt down a glass and grab water from the fridge's water dispenser. She was temporarily distracted by the wine fridge in front of her before she continued to search for the water she wanted.

Thankfully, her thinking didn't even get that far because there were bottles of water in the fridge. In fact, the refrigerator was fully stocked with fruits, vegetables, various meats, and dairy products. It had probably enough food to feed ten people, if not more, versus just her and Garrett. A quick glance at a couple of items told her none of the food looked to be expired. So, did someone regularly restock the food or had they known she was coming? She took a second to explore a couple of the cabinets and found some nonperishables, but before she could explore any further, Jules heard someone clear their throat behind her.

"Having fun?"

She paused her movements before she turned around, bottle of water in hand. As she turned around, she said, "Just exploring a bit. Is it normal for safe houses to have every food imaginable?"

"I'm not sure. I only know what Knox does."

Jules looked at him for a moment before walking out of the kitchen to head down the hall to the bedroom. As she was walking past Garrett, she felt his hand lightly grasp her wrist, stopping her in her tracks. She looked down at where the bodies were connected before her gaze made its way back up to his.

"You know we need to talk about what happened."

"Do you mean all this? I know about as much as you do."

"No. About what happened after I left."

Jules stared at him, refusing to shift her gaze. "Now you

want to talk about something? No, you don't set the parameters this time. We'll talk about it when I'm ready. If I'm ever ready."

Jules snatched her wrist out of his grasp. Rapidly retracing his steps, she closed the door to the bedroom, shutting the world and Garrett out. And she cried.

9

Sometimes there was nothing a good cry couldn't fix. Or that was what Jules told herself as she stared down at her phone while sitting on the side of the bed. It had been forty-five minutes since she'd left Garrett in the hallway of the safe house, and she'd managed to send a quick text to her parents saying she'd call later before descending into tears. With a heavy heart, she clicked a few buttons, before placing the phone to her ear.

"Jules, there you are." The concern in her mother's voice made her feel worse. Sadness overtook her as she realized she'd worried them.

Jules rubbed the back of her neck. "I know. I tried calling you earlier, but it just went to voicemail. I would have called again, but with everything going on I—"

Her words halted as she was overcome with emotion once again. She had been able to keep it together for several minutes before trying to call her parents. Jules took a deep breath and tried again.

"Sweetheart?"

Her mother's soothing voice floated through the speaker. She wished they could be together right now.

"Are you both okay?"

"We are, sweetheart." Her mother's response caused a smidge of worry to lift from her weary heart.

"We're still at home, but have security in place and are ready to move if anything changes. Garrett mentioned that he was taking you to a Knox-owned safe house when he gave me an update."

That brought her to the next point of this call. "Dad, there's a lot of things that I need answers to."

"I know." His voice joined her mother's on the call.

"How'd all this start, and why did you call Garrett?"

William sighed. "There's a lot that has happened that I haven't told you."

"That's an understatement." Her voice didn't waver that time as she worked hard to keep her emotions in check.

"I'm being blackmailed into revealing something I've supposedly done."

"So, take it to the police?"

"I wish it were so simple."

Jules shook her head slightly, and her gaze narrowed as she tried to understand what her father was trying to say. "Which part of that is complicated?"

"All of it. I don't know what I did to cause all of this and just going to the police is not as simple as it sounds."

"Let's start from the beginning." Hopefully doing so would provide some clarity to the situation for Jules.

"A few weeks ago, we started getting random phone calls on our home phone. The person would hang up almost immediately, and I've tried to have someone trace the call, but we got nowhere."

"Of course, things wouldn't be that easy," Jules said.

"Unfortunately."

"That's not all. Continue, William."

Jules imagined her mother grabbing her father's hand and giving it a quick squeeze, letting him know he had her full support. She'd seen her mom do it several times over the years and noticed the calming effect it had on him.

"Well, this evening I got a letter saying if I didn't come clean, I would lose my pride and joy." Jules remembered that line from when Garrett had told her what was going on while they were driving back to her apartment. "I knew the person had to be talking about you or Sebastian. Although I was worried about our safety, my main priority was you, so I called in the best of the best."

"And the best was Garrett?" Jules was proud of herself for keeping her voice neutral.

"Yes, and that's outside of Knox's stellar reputation. Plus, you guys grew up together practically, so I knew there was some trust there."

'Was' was the operative word in his statement. Jules could go over in her mind all the times that she and Garrett's twin sisters had tried to follow behind him, copying the things he used to do. They probably annoyed him, but he didn't show it much, unless it involved having to babysit them on occasion. Her own brother, Sebastian, was several years older, so the age gap played a role in why they weren't as close to one another. There was also the fact that Sebastian and William seemed to butt heads more often than not, but Jules refused to tell her mother that she thought that was probably one of the reasons why he didn't come home as much.

"Does Sebastian have any protection too? Just in case?"

"He does."

Her father's tone and him not elaborating told her not to push that line of questioning further. So, she changed the subject. "Can you tell me more about Knox?"

Her father didn't say anything for a moment. The silence sounded as loud as thunder before it broke. "Knox is a top-security firm, and they work with some of the biggest names in the world. I'd heard about Knox through the grapevine, and Terry confirmed that Garrett was a Knox agent."

"Why didn't you tell me Garrett worked for them?"

"You never asked."

That was a good point. She'd stopped talking to and about Garrett after he'd left so she couldn't blame her father for not bringing it up.

"I'll follow up with Garrett, but there is one thing I haven't mentioned." Jules went on to tell her experience with the birthday card.

"You should have shared that with us too, sweetheart," Carol added.

Jules knew her mother was right, but she'd written it off as a silly prank because she didn't have much to go on. She still wasn't sure it was connected to anything going on now, but things were leaning in that direction. Her eyes widened. Had the card turned up while Knox was picking up the wreckage in her apartment? She'd need to follow up with Garrett about that, she guessed.

"Dad, you didn't talk about the screaming match that happened not too long ago? I walked to your office to make sure that everything was okay... I think it was the same week I came over for dinner."

"Oh, I don't think that was related."

"Still suspicious in my eyes. What was that all about?"

"It was just Ellis Washington. He was upset over a decision that would further focus the direction of the foundation. Isn't the first time, won't be the last. I usually just let him get his frustrations out, and we decide how to proceed from there."

Jules didn't interact with Ellis very often, but when she did, it was a frosty reception. She'd mention that to Garrett as well.

"Jules, we are going to try to get some rest, although I know it'll be hard to come by. If you need anything, please reach out. We'll move past this threat soon."

"I know, Mom. Thank you. I'll talk to you both soon."

"We love you."

"And I love you."

Once her parents hung up, Jules debated whether it was worth turning in for the night or going to talk to Garrett. Curiosity won, and before she could compute what her body was doing, she found her feet taking her to the door.

Before turning the knob, Jules noticed the dull light under the door, possibly from the hallway, so there was a chance that Garrett was still awake. She opened the door softly and pulled the door to her. Once she'd taken a few steps down the hall, she found Garrett sitting on the couch with his laptop in front of him and the television played silently in the living room.

What she hadn't been expecting was to find him shirtless. She couldn't deny that she didn't want to stare at his muscular frame as his gaze was focused on whatever was on the screen in front of him. Thankfully, the darkness that mostly surrounded her due to the lack of light in the room hadn't revealed her location to him.

"Do you need something? I baked some chicken thighs and roasted veggies if you want any. It's in the fridge," he asked her without looking up from his computer.

Jules tried to hide the blush that was fighting its way to her cheeks as he proved her wrong.

"Wait, do you still eat meat? I should have asked that earlier."

"I do. I'll probably grab some of it, thanks. I wanted to talk to you about what happened tonight."

Garrett finally glanced up from his computer, giving her his full and undivided attention. He placed his laptop on the coffee table in front of him, stood up, and stretched, giving her a better view of just how hard he worked on his body. He'd been in decent shape when they were younger, but it was nothing compared to the work of art standing in front of her. The dark sweatpants hanging low on his hips almost made her stop breathing, wondering if there was a chance they might dip lower. The desire to run her hand along his muscular stomach was there, but she swallowed it. Jules was wandering into dangerous territory, and she needed to get out of it.

She let her gaze leave his body as they both walked toward the kitchen. Their hands grazed one another just before Garrett allowed her to walk in front of him. He turned on the light, illuminating the kitchen as Jules went over to the fridge to pull out the food he'd prepared. When she had the

Tupperware container in hand, she turned around and found he'd set out a fork and bowl for her.

"Thank you."

He shrugged, and she prepared the food to be reheated in the microwave. When she turned back around to face him once the food was reheating, he stared back at her, unabashedly. His gaze made her feel warm, yet unsure at the same time. She couldn't let anything he was doing deter her from her main focus.

"When Knox searched my apartment, did they find a birthday card of any sort? One that looked like it was made for a child?"

Garrett looked away for a second before his eyes met hers. "I looked through the inventory list but didn't remember seeing any photos or reading any descriptions that contained that. Why?"

Jules told her story for the second time that evening and stopped when the microwave beeped.

"I think you're right to be suspicious about the card. Let me double check that I didn't see it, but nonetheless, I'll have Knox take a look into it."

He left the room and quickly returned, with his laptop in tow. She ate and watched on in silence as he worked to find the answer. When she swallowed another bite, she said, "Find it?"

Garrett shook his head. "Not yet."

His search continued, and Jules stopped eating to grab something to drink out of the fridge. When she returned to her food, Garrett let out a grunt. "You okay?"

"Yes. Just annoyed that it's not there. And you're sure you didn't throw it away?"

"Positive. I was still hoping to find out who sent it, so I kept it."

"Well, it seems like whoever trashed your apartment took it with them. But for what reason, I'm not sure."

"There's something else I should add. A week or two ago I heard someone yelling at my father over the phone. When I confronted my dad about it, he said that it was Ellis Washington and that sometimes he did things like that but would elaborate on why he was yelling."

"Who is Ellis?"

"He's on the foundation's board of directors."

Garrett nodded, his expression even more serious than before. "I'll follow up with your father about it."

When Jules opened her eyes the next morning, she rose with a start. Her pounding heart was synchronized with the thoughts careening through her mind as she tried to figure out where she was. The grogginess started to fade, and it took a moment before she was able to replay the events that happened last night and place together her location.

She was in the lone bedroom of the apartment she'd been brought to after hers was destroyed. She and Garrett had talked for a few more minutes about where the birthday card could be but had agreed there was no use in stressing out about it overnight, because there wasn't anything they could do about it. She'd sent him the photos she had taken of the card, before washing the dishes she'd dirtied and headed back into the bedroom.

That was almost the last thing Jules had remembered because she quickly prepared herself for bed and eventually fell asleep after tossing and turning. Although she woke up several times throughout the night, Jules was happy that was the least of her worries right now because she was safe while this person was still on the loose.

Jules got out of bed and immediately went to the bathroom to brush her teeth. She'd figured the least she could do was make sure she didn't have morning breath when she ran into Garrett. Although the anger with him was still there, she made a deal with herself that she could remain civil during the time they had to spend together. Once this was over, she'd go back to living her life and he'd go back to living his.

Jules checked her phone when she walked back into the bedroom. After deciding not to read any more text messages the evening before, she checked her notifications and found only two. She was somewhat puzzled by it. because she'd assumed that her phone would be blowing up, but it seemed as if the people who knew what was going on had kept it quiet.

Rae: Hey, Garrett and Flint talked and updated us on what was going on. I told Liv and Eve and we're going to let you rest. We're trying to remain calm about everything but know that you need less stress. Reach out when you're up for it.

The kind text message made Jules' eyes water, but she was able to keep it together. Having such good friends all the time, let alone when you're going through one of the worst things that had ever happened to you, was truly special. She clicked over to the next notification.

Sebastian: Jules, Mom called and said what is going on. Text me to let me know you're okay.

She didn't expect the message from her brother at all, so that was a welcomed surprise.

Jules: I'm fine, but I'm currently in lockdown. Don't know when all of this will be over. How are you doing?

She checked the time and saw that chances were, Sebastian would still be asleep.

Grabbing a sweater from the suitcase she had haphazardly packed last night, Jules tossed it on over her tank top and pajama bottoms, before opening the door. As soon as she crossed the threshold, smells of food being cooked hit her nose. She walked toward the kitchen and found Garrett, wearing a t-shirt and shorts, in front of the stove. Getting a better look at the appliances in the kitchen told her that Knox had spent a pretty penny on them.

"You must love cooking." She gave herself a pat on the back for the small talk and the 'polite mask' that was stationed on her face as soon as she left the bedroom.

He looked over his shoulder at her, acknowledging that she'd entered the room. "Good morning. And everyone needs to eat, so it didn't hurt to learn."

"Is this some training that Knox provides?"

Garrett glanced at her for a split second, the look on his face asked if she was serious. "Hardly. There is some training in regard to food and survival, but nothing about regular cooking."

"What made you want to join Knox?" See? Still a somewhat neutral topic.

"I liked their mission and what they stood for. Kane actually connected me with the people there, and I went through all of the rigorous training and tests to make sure that I was right for the job."

She knew he was simplifying it for her benefit, but what he was saying was still impressive. Didn't change her feelings toward him, but he'd clearly done well.

"So, I see you have fulfilled your goal of working for your family's foundation."

She could deal with the small talk. "I have. It's fun, for the most part. I love being able to help those who are in need. The political arm of the foundation can be where things get more hectic. Thankfully, I don't touch that side too often, outside of the communication items which need to be completed for both sides."

"Understandable how things could get complicated on the political end."

"That's an understatement."

Garrett chuckled, and the sound was foreign to her ears. Most of the time she'd spent around him, even when they were younger, he was being cocky, sarcastic, or very serious. The change was jarring and exemplified just how much she didn't know about the man he'd grown to be.

"Jules." Her name sounded like a melody as it came from his lips. He shut the stove top off, removing the fried eggs he'd just prepared.

"Mhm?"

"We have some developments about last night, but you should sit down first before we talk about it."

Her stomach dropped to her toes. His tone told her it wouldn't be good news, and she didn't know if she was mentally prepared for it. Jules took her time grabbing the breakfast Garrett had prepared and sat down at the dining room table. Garrett handed her a glass of juice before he went back into the kitchen to get his own food. She took a sip of the orange juice as he settled into his own seat.

"What did you want to tell me?"

"It might be wise to stay here longer than a couple of days."

"Wait. Why?" Jules said slowly, as she wanted to know where he was going with this. "I thought Knox was processing my apartment, and I would be able to go home within a couple of days."

"Knox is doing a thorough job of checking for any evidence the suspect might have left behind, and we've also hired an outside service that has been thoroughly vetted to help put your apartment back together. Our main concern now is the security vulnerabilities at your building. This person was able to get past your doorman, and the limited security measures the owner of your building has in place, in order to break-in and destroy your things. What if you'd been there when the suspect had entered?"

Jules had thought about that angle, and it frightened her. She might have been defenseless against someone who threatened her life. The other option might be to have Garrett stay with her, but that felt weird having him in her space. She didn't trust him completely, and all of this was happening so fast. This safe house felt more like a neutral ground, although she wasn't completely comfortable.

"I'm glad it's being addressed. Hopefully things will be rectified by the time we leave here. I hope it's sooner rather than later. I can't wait to get back to my life."

Her words caused him to drop the utensil he was holding and stare at her. "Are you taking this seriously? Someone threatened your life and destroyed your apartment, letting you know they know where you live. Hell, they also probably know where you work, where your barre studio is, and where you go grocery shopping as well. It's clear whoever did this knows a lot about you, and if they wanted to, could have probably already killed you. They didn't have to wait until you were out with your friends to enter your apartment, Jules."

That led Jules to snap. "Don't you think I know that! I understand the ramifications, but I don't want to live in fear, constantly looking over my shoulder, wondering when this person is going to kill me. I don't need you to explain it to me."

The coldness that seeped from the last words she said elicited a glare from Garrett, but she didn't finch under his gaze. "Then stop thinking that you are invincible."

"When have I ever thought that? There are some things that I thought would last, but I never thought that I was."

She used those words intentionally, a slight dig at the last time she spoke to him.

"Jules, I—"

"Garrett, I asked you not to call me Jules. Please respect that and my wishes. I'll stay here as long as I have to, but I don't want to talk about anything else."

She could see that he wanted to say something else, but he refrained. It was clear that he knew that saying something else would just make things worse. Jules stood up, appetite gone, and took her plate and glass to the kitchen. When she was done clearing it up, she walked back into the bedroom without another word to him.

11

J ules rubbed her hands across her face, giving in to the sensation to take a break. She had been on the phone or answering emails for the last couple of hours. The strain of working along with the other stressors she was dealing with were starting to take their toll, coupled with everything else going on. She would be so happy not only once the threats on her life were over, but also once this gala she was trying to put together was complete as well. And just a few days ago, it was the biggest thing she had to worry about. Oh, how quickly things could change.

Everyone was doing their best to keep the current state of affairs quiet, so it didn't leak out and do any damage to anyone publicly. Having the added stress of the public trying to figure out or want to know more about what was happening might just be Jules' undoing.

Jules moved her laptop, which had been resting on her lap, and stretched her arms up while rolling her neck. That was one thing she could do. It had been a while since she had gone to a barre class, and she was happy that her studio offered classes on demand. She got up off the bed and looked through the drawers to find some gym clothes — happy she'd remembered to bring them through the chaos of dealing with the disaster zone that was her apartment. Jules quickly changed and walked into the living room area to cross into the kitchen to grab a bottle of water. It came as no surprise that Garrett was leaning over his own computer and looked up when she entered the room.

Jules could feel his gaze on her, and it was probably due to her outfit which consisted of a sports bra and leggings. "What are you doing?"

"What does it look like I'm doing?"

Garrett smirked before he said, "I know something that would give you better work out than the one you're about to do."

Jules closed the refrigerator door before slamming the water bottle down the counter. She easily read the deeper meaning behind his words, and he had some nerve to even insinuate it. Before she could snap at him, she stopped herself. "Why don't you join me in this workout?"

Garrett leaned back in his chair. "Are you sure? I don't want to show you up while you're doing your routine."

Jules let out a belly laugh that somewhat shocked even her. She usually kept those kinds of expressions of emotion under wraps, unless she was around people she trusted, and right now, she knew she didn't trust Garrett as far as she could throw him. "There's no way you're beating me at a barre workout. If this isn't something you do regularly, it can be rigorous for a first timer."

"I can handle it." Confidence oozed out Garrett's statement as he moved his chair back and stood up. "But there is something I want you to do for me, if I make it through the entire workout."

"Oh yeah?"

"I want to talk to you about what happened right after I graduated from college. I'm hoping that you'll let me explain my side to you and apologize. If you choose to accept my apology, that's great. If you don't, that's fine. I just want to tell you my side of things."

Jules' eyes shifted away from Garrett as she thought about his proposal. "Deal."

Maybe having him explain his point of view would help her to move on from the resentment that she had against him. But she wasn't going to let him have his way easily. "We can stream my workout to the TV, right? It would probably be easier to see on a bigger screen than my laptop."

"I don't see why not. Why don't I get that set up while you go grab your laptop? I'll set it up and then go change, and we should be good to go."

Jules nodded, and Garrett walked over to the TV to figure out if watching the barre workouts would be possible. She turned on her heel and walked back to her bedroom, a smile playing on her face. She already knew which workout she was going to pick, and she couldn't wait to see the expression on his face once the session was complete.

"AND THAT'S A WRAP," the instructor on the television's screen explained while clapping. "Congrats on finishing this barre workout. We hope you enjoyed your time with us, and we can't wait to see you again real soon."

Jules smiled wide, happy that she had just accomplished this workout. It was one she had done a few times before in hopes that each time she did, she would get better at the moves the instructor was encouraging them to do.

"Wow. That was... something."

Jules looked over at Garrett who was currently reclined back on the floor, arms holding him up. They had been doing a floor routine, and it was clear the workout was more challenging than he had expected. She had to admit she was pretty impressed with Garrett's ability to keep up with the barre class. "How are you doing over there?"

"I'm alive."

Jules snorted before covering her mouth. She gaped at him before a few giggles came out of her mouth, but the sound was muffled by her hands, once again breaking character with her emotions. It seemed Garrett had her doing a whole lot of things that she normally didn't do when he reentered her life. "I didn't expect you to do the whole routine."

"Well, I had some extra motivation to get the job done." His eyes stayed glued to her. "I really want to explain my side of the story. It doesn't have to be right now, but I was determined to do it before we leave the little bubble we are in."

"That's fine. You made it through the class, so I'll keep up my end of the bargain."

Garrett nodded his head and attempted to get up but failed. "I will never doubt how difficult or effective your barre classes are again."

"Good. Do you want to do another one some time? You seemed to be enjoying it."

"If it means taking it again with you, then yes."

Jules knew she was setting herself up for an answer like

the one he just gave as the words flew out of her mouth. Still, she hadn't been expecting that response. She licked her lips before standing up. The familiar ache that dictated a good barre workout crept into her body as she maneuvered upright. Although she was sore from the workout as well, it was clear her body was more conditioned to perform the moves and recover more quickly than Garrett's was. It was understandably so, given how often and long she had taken classes versus him.

She walked over to where he was laying and held her hand out. His eyes shifted from her face to her hand and back to her face before he put his hand in hers. The warmth yet firmness of his touch shocked her, almost making her wish that she could feel his fingertips in more places on her body. She wondered if he, too, felt as if this might have been a turning point in their reunion and that things were only going to go up from here. Then again, based on the luck she was having, it seemed as if things were only going to go from bad to worse.

12

"**G**lad we could get everyone together for this meeting. It's great to meet you, Juliana, although I wish it were under better circumstances."

Jules nodded in response. "Likewise."

Both Garrett and Jules were staring at his laptop on the coffee table, waiting for Maverick to continue. Garrett mentioned Maverick was the founder of Knox and had recruited him to join the company after Kane had recommended him. Although she could only see part of him, it was easy to tell he also took his fitness very seriously, and she thought it made sense given his line of work, and he'd probably want to set a good example for his team. His long blond hair was tied back in a ponytail, and she watched as the friendly expression that had been on his face when he had greeted her turned more serious.

"We have some good news and some bad news."

"Please go with the good news." Jules thought everyone could use this first, even if the bad news was worse than she thought it could be.

"We have a couple of leads on the man who ransacked your place."

"Oh, that's such good news," her mom interjected before Maverick could continue. She watched as her father patted his wife on the hand and Jules smiled at their interaction.

"There were a couple of fingerprints that we found at the scene of the crime that we were able to trace back to an individual. We have eyes on him, in case he does get spooked and tries to skip town, but once we are completely sure that he is the one who did it, we'll bring him in."

"And the bad news?" William chimed in.

Jules was happy to have her parents on the call because it meant they were safe and sound. It was also another opportunity to see their faces, as they were heavily involved as well.

"What we don't know is if he's the one that threatened your life. Even if he isn't, we'd be one step closer to finding out who is."

Jules nodded, pleased with the development. Honestly, she hadn't been expecting things to be moving as quickly as they were, but she was grateful. "Mom, Dad, have you heard from Sebastian at all? Shouldn't we be somewhat worried about whether or not this person might go after him as well?"

Garrett jumped in this time and said, "Sebastian is completely safe in California, and we are ready to make adjustments to that plan if it comes down to it."

A brief look of what Jules thought was puzzlement crossed Maverick's face before he continued, "William, are you sure you can't think of anything that would cause someone to want to attack you or your family? Having any type of motive right now is crucial and could lead to us finding out who this person is."

Jules watched as her father thought about Maverick's comment before he responded.

"Nope. As far as I know, I don't have any enemies. I'm sure there are some people in the world who don't like me, but enough to come after my family? No."

Maverick adjusted his monitor so everyone could see him clearer. "As we've said before, if you could think of anything, let us know immediately. The more we all know, the better we can prepare for anything that might occur."

The undertone in his voice told her that he meant something more dangerous than having her apartment torn to shreds. She didn't know if she'd ever get over someone doing that to her place, and the violation still felt too real. Her mind was almost made up in terms of finding somewhere else to live once this was all said and done. Jules knew she was meant to feel safe in her own home, and even though it was days after the attack, the wound that was created by having her things destroyed was still huge.

"Thanks so much for the update. I'm glad things are developing quickly in the right direction."

"You're welcome. Oh, before everyone goes, there's one thing that I want to say."

Everyone stopped moving and waited for Maverick to continue.

"Jules, you are in the best care with Garrett at your side. He is one of the best on my team, and I probably shouldn't say this with him sitting next to you because it will go to his head."

Jules chuckled as a smirk formed on Garrett's face.

"Thanks, boss."

"And that's why I wanted him to protect Jules. I only wanted the best for my daughter."

Jules felt the smile leave her face and could feel herself tearing up at her father's words, but she was able to hold it together. She didn't want to start crying in front of an audience.

"Okay, we'll keep each other in the loop, and hopefully, we have some good news in the next forty-eight to seventy-two hours or so."

"Talk to you soon," Garrett said before he disconnected the call. He then turned to Jules once he closed his laptop. "That wasn't so bad."

"No, it was pretty good news, actually." In the back of her mind sat Maverick's words about this suspect potentially not being the man who actually wants to harm her. What if it was a team of people that wanted her dead? Jules swallowed hard and ran her hand through her long strands before looking at Garrett.

Garrett's eyes followed her hand as it made its way to the end of her hair before his eyes shot back to hers. "What's on your mind?"

"What do you mean?"

"Although the call was pretty short—not surprising since Maverick doesn't beat around the bush—it was a lot to take in. How are you doing?"

"I'm fine."

"Don't lie to me."

Although his words were a bit harsh, the tone he used when he said them showed her he didn't mean it that way. His hand slid down and cupped her cheek softly. The warmth from his fingers lit something inside of her that she thought she had buried when he'd left her behind all of those years ago, yet here she was, trying to prevent herself from leaning into his touch.

"Garrett, I swear. I'm fine."

"And I know you're not. The face you chose to show to the public, the one that you like to wear so that no one can see what you're really thinking about? Doesn't work on me. I watched your expression as you took in the news that Maverick laid out in front of everyone on the call. And you have every right to be upset. So don't hide your feelings around me. You've done nothing wrong."

Jules knew he was right and could feel the dam that was holding her feelings back begin to crack. "I know I haven't, but bad things happen to people who don't do anything to deserve it all the time."

"I know."

Jules let out a deep breath and leaned back on the couch with her eyes closed. She took a few more breaths as she tried to calm herself down. How she wasn't on track to having a panic attack with everything going on around her she didn't know. Even though her eyes were closed, she could still feel the weight of Garrett's gaze on her, watching her every move. The sensation provided a sense of security yet made her nervous. What exactly was he doing to her?

"Jules, you don't have to be strong all of the time."

Garrett's comment took her aback and her eyes swung open.

"I—" The words died on her lips because she realized she didn't have a response. He was right. She'd done her best to portray this perfect image to the world so no one would know her real feelings on many matters. After all, the spotlight had been on her to be perfect, and Jules never wanted to embarrass her family or ruin her family's legacy. But right now, there was no one here, besides them, and she could feel herself falling back into the rhythm they had developed when they were younger. How much she'd longed for him to be her confidant over the years, but her mind refused to reach out to him due to the hurt he had caused her.

"I keep trying to rationalize things with myself that it's things that can be easily replaced due to the privileges I have, but I just can't shake how hurt I am." Tears sat at the corners of her eyes, and she sniffled. She didn't want to cry because she had done so much over the last several days, but she couldn't help it. She angrily swiped the tears that dared to fall.

Garrett leaned forward and pushed a piece of her hair back behind her ear. The warm gesture almost made her smile through the tears. "We're going to get whoever is doing this, and no one is going to hurt you on my watch, okay?"

Jules nodded her head, staring down at her fingers as they played with the ends of her hair.

"If they even try, I will make sure that is the last thing that they do."

Jules looked back up at him and knew he meant every word. And the thought of that made her feel both safe and terrified at the same time.

13

"Thank goodness today is Friday," Jules mumbled as she finished typing an email. She was double checking the numbers for who was scheduled to attend the Cartwright Foundation Gala and sending an email to the caterer. To be honest, she hoped she was sending this email late enough in the day to guarantee the caterer wouldn't email her back until Monday.

Once she pressed send, Jules looked around and stretched. She couldn't believe she had now spent over a week in this safehouse with Garrett. For the most part, things had been going well, although she still felt bad he had to sleep on the couch in the living room. He didn't complain at all, however.

The ringing of her phone made Jules nearly jump off the bed. She had turned her ringer on while she was waiting for a grantee to call her and hadn't remembered to turn it off. She crossed her fingers in her mind that it wasn't someone else trying to call her about work, due to it being just a few minutes before the weekend was set to begin. Jules could have jumped for joy when she saw Liv's number pop up on the screen. She hurried and answered the call.

"I'm so happy it's you and not someone else calling from work. I'm officially checked out."

"Well, it's all three of us, and I'm happy to be of service."

Jules chuckled as Rae and Eve greeted her. "Hey to you all too."

"We just called to check in on you since we haven't been able to see you in person for a while. I know how it feels to be away from everyone you care about for a long time," Eve said.

Jules knew that to be true and remembered when Eve had left town to stay with Kane when things were dangerous for her to be in the D.C. At least Jules could say she was still in D.C., although no one knew where she was, besides what she assumed were members of Knox and herself.

"I appreciate the check-in, you guys, I really do." Jules gave them the rundown of the latest that was going on in the race to find out who wanted to harm her. "I'm hoping to have more information soon, but that's where things stand as of now."

"I'm glad Knox is working quickly to get this person...or people."

Jules was able to smile at Rae's words. "I feel the same way."

"Speaking of Garrett..."

"Liv, there's no need to badger her about him."

"Thanks, Eve."

Liv scoffed. "Oh, come on. Don't tell me you all weren't thinking about it too."

Rae chuckled. "Of course we were. We just didn't have enough confidence to throw it out there like you did."

"So, what you're saying is that you should be thanking me."

Eve sighed in response. "Only you would take that as a sign to give thanks for something."

Liv paused for a moment. "Thank. You. Anyway, we are getting off track here. How are things with Garrett, Jules?"

The strong emphasis on her name told everyone on the call the only person she wanted to hear from was the person in question. Jules also knew that she was about to be disappointed but shared her answer anyway.

"Things are good. We're getting along, and everything is very calm."

"No fighting?"

"Nope."

"No kissing?"

"Nada." Jules had to admit, this was kind of fun.

"No sex?"

"I think that was implied with the no kissing part," Rae added.

"You can do the dirty without kissing."

Before Liv could go any further, Jules said, "We have been essentially acting like roommates who get along."

"Sometimes roommates bang as well."

"Liv..." Eve's voice was full of warning.

"Seriously? I'm shocked."

Jules held back the laugh that was bubbling in her stomach. She couldn't lie to fill Liv's desire to have something to talk about.

The truth was that things had been pretty quiet between

Garrett and herself. She would have assumed that he wanted to keep things strictly professional if she hadn't noticed the heated looks he gave her every so often that made her question why didn't she just say to hell with it and have sex with him to get it both out of their systems? After all, it wasn't something they ever acted on when they were younger, and they were both adults now and could handle a little fooling around. It would diffuse some of the tension she felt whenever they were in the same room.

"Earth to Jules."

Jules coughed lightly when she heard Rae call her name. "I'm here. What's up?"

The rest of the conversation went smoothly as each woman talked about what was new in their lives. Before Jules knew it, Eve mentioned that she had to go, so the women decided to end the call. When Jules hung up, she couldn't help but smile. Even with Liv's light badgering, she missed being able to talk to her friends and see them in person. Yes, even when it was easy for them to get together, they sometimes went a few weeks without seeing each other due to their busy schedules, but right now not having the ability to do it at all sucked more. But Jules was willing to take what she could get and talking to them had forced a bright spot to grow in her day.

A knock on the bedroom door shifted her attention, and she told the only person who it could be to come in.

"Hey," she said softly when Garrett opened the door.

Garrett gave her a smile in return. "I was just checking in on you. Heard you talking on the phone."

"Liv, Rae and Eve called to check up on me, and I'm happy that they did."

"Great. Well, let me know if you need anything."

Liv's questioning flew through Jules' mind at rapid speed as she thought about the time she and Garrett had spent together the last week and before she could stop herself, she said, "Hey, are you starting to get hungry? I could cook something."

Garrett leaned on the doorjamb and looked at her, a grin slowly forming. "I could eat."

She had to admit that he'd done a lot of the cooking for them while they'd been staying here, and sometimes she would just quickly grab the food and bring it into her bedroom so she could continue working. But this evening, she vowed to shake things up.

"Awesome, I'll get started in a few minutes." She stood up to stretch her legs, but his follow up question stopped her movement.

"Could I do anything to help?"

It was a combination of his question and the way he asked it that forced her to pause and quickly gather her thoughts. "Uh—maybe. Let me see what food we have left, and then I can figure out if I need any help."

"We're fully stocked. Food delivery from Knox came a few hours ago."

Jules knew her confusion must have been written all over her face. "How did I miss that?"

"I heard you on the phone just before it came."

"Ah okay, well let's see what we have and then let's get to cooking."

∽

"JUST A FEW MORE MINUTES AND everything should be ready," Jules announced when she put the lid back on the pot. She reached over and grabbed her phone to check the time as she saw Garrett out of the corner of her eye, digging into one of the cabinets. "Why didn't you just stay in a safe house that Knox provides while your apartment is getting ready?"

"That was random."

"I know, and I'm being extremely nosey. I apologize."

"No harm done. Honestly, I wanted to spend more time with Flint because we haven't seen each other in a long time. I also hadn't met Rae in person either, so that was another advantage. One of the best ways to do that would be to stay with them for a little while, and they agreed."

"Make sense," Jules said as her head moved back down to her phone. In her peripheral vision, she could see Garrett placed the two wine glasses that he found in front of him and reached over to grab the bottle of wine.

"I assume you want some?"

When she looked up, he gestured to the bottle in his hand, she nodded. "Without a doubt."

Garrett chuckled as he grabbed a corkscrew from another drawer and soon had the bottle open. Jules looked back down at her phone while he poured the glass of wine. She found herself checking her schedule for the next week and muttered a curse.

"What's wrong?" He handed the glass to her.

She took a sip and let the wine sit in her mouth for a moment before swallowing. "I just noticed I have a fundraiser to go to in a few days."

"This is not shocking information. I'm surprised it hasn't come up sooner."

Jules stared at Garrett with her eyebrow raised.

He smiled at her and lifted his glass before his expression turned serious. "If it's too dangerous for you to go, you're not going."

"Garrett, you can't make me do anything I don't want to do. This is my job."

"And my job is to protect you from whoever is trying to threaten to kill you. Is this fundraiser worth risking your life?"

The question he posed wasn't one that needed to be answered, but she did anyway. "I'm not willing to put my life in danger, but it would look strange if neither my father nor I were there. We are headliners at the event."

"You could just say a family emergency came up."

"And that would get people talking. You know how that circle runs just as much as I do." And he did, having grown up in it himself. "Wait, what if you went with me?"

"Like a date?"

Jules rolled her eyes. "Hardly, and it's not like you to be intentionally clueless. We'd just go there together and keep me safe. See? We both win."

"And what are you going to tell the people running the event when I show up there with you?"

That was an easy question. "That you're my guest."

"And you don't think that would force all eyes on us if the gossipy set is there?"

Jules groaned. Once again, he was right. "How about we just let everyone assume whatever they are going to assume? After all, it is none of their business anyway."

"You're right about that. Cheers."

14

"Why haven't you taken off from work?"

"W-wait what?" Garrett's question startled Jules.

"With everything that is going on, I was curious as to why you hadn't taken off from work. I'm sure your father would have been more than understanding about it." Garrett took a sip from his glass of water. It was a couple of hours after they'd finished dinner, and they were both relaxing on the couch, enjoying one another's company. Soft music was coming out of the television speakers, setting a soothing mood between the two. This had been the longest they'd spoken to one another in years, and Jules had to admit that it was nice.

She was determined to ignore the elephant in the room, and it had to do with the unfinished business they had from years ago. No, she wasn't going to let that ruin the moment they were currently sharing.

Jules tossed Garrett's question around in her head in an

attempt to answer it truthfully. The coldness that she felt toward him was thawing rapidly over the time they spent together, and Jules couldn't tell if it was due to her trying to heal from the emotional scars that had formed as a result of her anger toward him or to their close proximity to one another and she was doing this as a sign or a coping mechanism. She hoped it was the former and not the latter.

Jules sighed and put her feet up underneath her. "Because it shows weakness. I'm sure you noticed that my father hasn't taken off either."

"I have. Has your father told you that it is a sign of weakness?"

Jules shook her head. "No, he hasn't."

"So, it's something that you've just taken on yourself."

"Garrett, don't try to psychoanalyze me right now."

Garrett put his hands up, showing that he meant no harm. "Not what I was trying to do at all. Just trying to get to know the adult you better."

Jules turned her head, looking at him straight on. "And why is that?"

Garrett lightly swung the glass in his hand and watched as the water drifted from side to side. "Because I missed out on a lot when I was away. I want to know more about you. The things you like, the things you don't. Every aspect of what makes you, you."

"You had that opportunity years ago, Garrett." The elephant was circling the couple, getting closer and closer.

"I know, and I missed it. I messed everything up. Part of it was being young and the other part of it was me being foolish." He leaned forward and put his glass down on the coffee table.

Jules watched his movements and waited until the water stopped moving in his cup before she spoke. "It's in the past now. Years have gone by, and we've both moved on."

"Please don't let that lie sit between us. I hated how things ended between us."

She did too, but she didn't want to voice her thoughts.

"There's one thing I've been waiting years to do."

Jules turned back to him. "What's that?" Her voice was barely above a whisper.

"This."

Garrett's hand grazed her jaw before cupping it as he brought his face closer to hers, bridging the distance between them. When his lips met hers, she sighed into the kiss, tension dissipating. She'd known she missed the touch of his lips on hers, but she didn't know how much until this very moment. They fell back into a rhythm that they knew a long time ago, and she couldn't stop the pure feeling of bliss.

The kiss started out soft before it grew more intense as her hands made their way toward his chest. She clenched his shirt in her grasp, willing him to come closer to her without saying a word. Jules felt his hands making their way toward her shirt when the shrilling ring of his phone stopped them both.

Garrett pulled away first. "This can't be real life."

"I'm sorry to confirm it is. You probably should grab that."

"I know, but I don't want to."

Jules chuckled. "It might be important."

Garrett groaned as Jules shook her head. He'd get over it. When he looked down at his phone, the groan stopped suddenly.

"Everything alright?"

"You're right, I definitely need to take this call." Garrett laid a quick peck on her lips before he stood up. "Hold that thought, though. Hopefully, this won't take too long."

He turned and headed toward the kitchen, she assumed in hopes of getting some privacy. She waited a few moments to see if he would come back, and when he didn't, she stood up to walk toward the bedroom. As she walked past the kitchen, he glanced up at her, but his expression was unreadable. She thought that whatever they had going on while they were on the couch was done as she crossed the threshold into the bedroom. Jules glanced at the bed before making her way into the master bathroom. When she flicked on the light, the first thing she did was look at herself in the mirror.

There stood a woman, who looked like she had been thoroughly kissed. Her blue eyes were slightly dilated, and her blonde hair was a wreck. If none of that had given it away, the light blush on her cheeks would have. Feeling the urge to calm her heated skin down, Jules turned on the faucet and ran some cool water along her fingertips before cupping her hand and tossing some of the water on her face. She reached over and grabbed a towel and patted her skin dry before replacing it. Just as she was about to turn around to head back into the bedroom, Garrett appeared in the doorway of the bathroom.

His eyes were wild, and she knew that their kiss hadn't been the only thing to put that look into his eyes.

"What happened? What's wrong?"

"We need to go."

"It's, like, nine o'clock. Where would we be going at this time of night?"

Garrett grabbed her hand and began pulling her in the direction of the doorway.

"Garrett, what's going on?"

Her voice stopped his forward movement. "They found the asshole who destroyed your apartment, and they are waiting for us to get there before the real questions begin."

15

J ules couldn't explain the knot forming in her stomach, but she could confirm that it was there. As Garrett drove them to a place that was owned by Knox, the nerves building in her stomach made her want to hurl. A way to keep herself from doing that was to keep quiet until they arrived.

She was happy Garrett respected her desire to keep her thoughts to herself, even though she hadn't told him that that was what she had wanted. His ability to read her mood at this time was a relief because she didn't have to say anything. No words, just the sound of the soft music Garrett put on danced between them in the car. It reminded her of the mood that had been broken just moments before with a phone call that shook her to her soul. Could this be the end of it? Would she be able to return to the life she knew soon?

But there was the lingering question of what her life would look like once she was able to get back to her routine. There was no way things would return back to the way they were before all of this had occurred. Thoughts clouded her mind about how she could regain the sense of security she'd had just a couple of weeks ago, but one thought that broke through the fog was about Garrett.

Her feelings about him had begun to shift the more time they spent together in the safe house, and now after the kiss they'd shared, things had snowballed toward her being able to trust him again. But what did the future look like for them outside of this?

Jules shook her head and looked out the passenger window as she tried to clear her thoughts. She needed to focus on what was happening now, and the future could be discussed at another time.

She turned to look at the man next to her and noticed the tightness of his jaw as his eyes were focused on the road in front of them. Maybe the silence was to his benefit as well. Tension radiated off of him, and she couldn't stop herself from saying something. "Are you okay?"

The simple question seemed to turn his mood upside down, because when he looked over at her, his expression completely changed. It was as if he was caught in his own world, and her words broke him out of the shell he had put himself in. "Yes, because I'm ready to get to the bottom of whoever is doing this to you. How are you feeling?"

Jules rested a hand on Garrett's leg momentarily, stopping his words. She could feel his gaze on her hand before looking back up at the road. "I don't know."

Her response caused Garrett to take a glimpse at her. "Why is that?"

"I feel...very vulnerable right now. And I didn't expect to." The mask that had become her safety net felt as if it had a large crater in it. Jules looked down at her hands before looking back up at Garrett. "How do you prepare yourself for something like this? I might be coming face to face with the person who is trying to have me killed. It's panic inducing."

"It's hard for me to tell you how to prepare for something like this. But I will say, he's not going to hurt you. I promise you that." Garrett held out his hand, and Jules put hers in his.

"I know. You wouldn't let it happen."

"WE HAVE the suspect in this room. He admitted to destroying the apartment." Jules saw Maverick glance at her out of the corner of her eye, but she didn't make eye contact with him. It wasn't due to the fact that he seemed even more intimidating and muscular in person, but it was due to the situation she was in. She was moments away from being face to face with the person who had helped destroy her life as she knew it.

Jules was trying to listen to the conversation Garrett and Maverick were having, but she was having a hard time focusing on much of anything. With her heart in her throat, a lot of the noise around her had mostly faded into the background.

"How did you finally confirm that it was him?" As Garrett said this, she lightly felt him touch her back. Although there was a lot they still needed to talk about, having him there made her feel better.

"He returned to her apartment...with another card."

"You're shitting me."

Maverick shook his head. "Wish I was."

The two were talking as if Jules wasn't standing there with

them, but she didn't mind. The information they were trading back and forth caused a dull ache to form inside of her heart. He'd come back to her apartment to potentially do further damage. She was even more grateful Garrett had really pushed the idea of her staying in a safe house for the time being. But with him being in Knox's custody, did that mean she could return home?

"What did the card say?" That was the first time Jules had said anything since they had driven onto Knox's private property.

Knox's headquarters had everything anyone would imagine when it came to being a security firm. From the levels of security that were needed to get into the building which included confirming Garrett's identity and him having to vouch for Jules and have her scanned for weapons, even though she was technically one of Knox's clients. It was clear they took security seriously, and although it was a minor inconvenience for her, she didn't mind. It provided a sense of comfort during a time of utter turmoil.

"Here we are," Maverick announced, ignoring Jules' question as the trio stopped outside of a door.

She waited a moment for either of them to say something, to tell her what was on the card, but neither seemed inclined to do so.

Maverick didn't even look at her, just kept his gaze on Garrett. "Do you want to handle this, or should I go in with you?"

"I can take it from here." Garrett replied and then turned to Jules and asked, "Do you want to go inside? If not, you don't have to. There's a room next to this one where you can watch without anyone knowing that you're there."

Going in there with whoever this person was made Jules nervous, and she could take the easier path and sit back and see what would happen during the interrogation. But would she end up regretting taking that approach in the end?

"I'll come in with you. I want to face this person head on."

Jules' response earned her a soft smile from Garrett. Although he didn't say anything out loud, she could see the pride shining in his eyes, making her feel warmer inside. That wasn't something she was expecting to feel just a week ago, but it was strange how things had changed in such a short amount of time. She was happy to feel more at peace with Garrett, but a nagging feeling still hung underneath the surface that she couldn't shake. She had made the decision she was going to talk to him about their past sooner rather than later.

With him leading the way, Jules followed him into the room where a lone man was sitting on a metal chair behind a metal desk. He looked a little worse for wear with his clothes somewhat torn and wrinkled, and Jules couldn't get a good look at his face because he was staring down at his hands. When Garrett cleared his throat, the man looked up, and his eyes darted between looking at Garrett and then looking at Jules. Finally, his eyes settled on her.

"Juliana."

"Yes? How do you know who I am?"

"He's talked about you."

Jules' blood turned to ice. She felt Garrett squeeze her hand lightly. This confirmed one of her biggest fears about this situation: that the person who'd threatened her life was still on the loose.

16

"What's your name?"

Garrett's question hung in the air as the couple waited for a response. Instead, the individual in front of them remained silent.

"We know that you have no problem hearing or speaking, so I will ask you one more time, what is your name?"

"Russell."

They were finally getting somewhere, although Jules' mind was still on Russell's earlier comment.

"What do you know about William Cartwright?"

Garrett's voice bounced off of the walls in the mostly empty room as Jules stared at the pathetic man in front of them. He looked around the room before his eyes settled on Jules. "I don't know him personally, but he's supposedly one of the biggest assholes who has ever lived in D.C."

Jules knew that his line of attack was meant to hurt her directly, but she didn't show any emotion. Somehow, she had gotten her emotions from earlier under control and kept her facial expression neutral. There was no way she was going to let Russell see that his words were affecting her.

"I highly doubt that to be the case. What do you have against him?"

Russell looked slightly taken aback by the question before a smirk filled with contempt and arrogance appeared on his face. As he crossed his arms, he said, "Nothing, because I'm not the person you need to worry about."

"Who hired you?" Jules' voice remained steady when she delivered her question, causing both men to turn to her. Her face remained expressionless, because there was no way she was going to let Russell tear her down.

"I don't have to tell you anything."

"See, that's where you're wrong. You're in Knox custody now, and it's in your best interest to tell us everything you know." Garrett leaned forward on the desk, daring Russell to say something to contradict what he said.

"Or what? I'm not afraid of you, her, or anyone else in this building."

"You should be. Because we have ways of doing things where no one would find your body for years. Is that what you want? I'm sure whoever hired you isn't paying you nearly enough to ever consider that thought."

Jules stopped her mouth from dropping open. The threat made her nervous, and it wasn't even directed at her.

"It's not about the money," Russell said.

Jules wasn't a psychologist, but she noticed that the cockiness had faded a fraction, and his eyes started to dart around the room once more. Garrett's threat had struck a chord.

"Then what is it about?" Garrett adjusted his body and looked even more muscular.

Jules wondered if he might reach across and slam this man's face into the table.

"It's about revenge and helping someone who helped me."

"Who hired you?" Jules asked again, hoping that this time he would give her an answer.

"I don't know."

"You don't know?" Garrett chimed in.

Although his voice remained steady, Jules glanced down and watched as he clenched and unclenched his fist. She wondered if he was going to take a swing at Russell.

Russell shook his head. "No. I was hired to destroy what I later learned to be her apartment and to deliver a couple of envelopes. That was all I did."

"And you just took money from a random person to do it?"

Russell scoffed. "When the price was right? Yes. I wasn't paid much, but it was enough to help me make ends meet."

Jules was taken aback by the admission. It shouldn't have come as a shock that someone with money was backing this operation, but given how vast her father's inner circle was, it could be anyone who might be holding a grudge.

"You know what? I'm done talking. I don't have anything else left to say except to wish you good luck." Staring directly into Jules' eyes, there was no doubt in her mind that his comment was directed specifically at her.

"You don't look okay."

Garrett's comment hit her like a truckload of bricks.

They'd been back at the safe house for just a few minutes before Jules walked into the bedroom and sat down on the edge of the bed. Jules looked up at him and found him standing in the doorway. Once again, an unreadable expression on his face.

She fought against her usual coping mechanism of burying her feelings but decided not to. "I don't know what I was expecting when we entered the room, other than the hope that this nightmare was over. And it's still not."

Garrett moved further into the room, sitting down next to her. "It's not, and I know you were really banking on Russell admitting to everything."

"Do you believe the things he said?"

"Yes. It's probably the only thing that saved him from getting punched in the face."

"Well, I'm glad you didn't."

"You are?"

Jules nodded. "I didn't want to have that on my conscience...nor did I want to have to jump out of the way of flying fists."

Garrett chuckled, and it made Jules smile for the first time in hours. Soon the smile turned into laughter which grew uncontrollable and forced Garrett to join in on the fun. Jules couldn't have predicted this change in mood even if she had tried.

Garrett stopped laughing first, and Jules soon followed as she wiped the tears that had formed in her eyes. She looked up at the man sitting to her right. "There's something you mentioned before we left that stuck with me throughout tonight's adventure."

"What was that?"

"When Maverick's call broke up our kiss, you told me to hold that thought. I'm still holding it, Garrett."

Recognition crossed over his features before his gaze made their way to her lips. "Are you sure about this? If so, this needs to remain between us, for now."

Jules nodded. "I haven't been more sure about anything else recently. I want to pick up where we left off and take our minds off of everything. Even if it's just for now." And she meant that with every fiber of her being.

"With pleasure."

Jules' heart thundered in her chest as she watched Garrett's face move closer to hers just before his lips touched her own.

The kiss started out soft before it grew in strength, a force to be reckoned with that took Jules by surprise. His hands grasped the sides of her face, begging her to come closer to him as their tongues intertwined. This was nothing like the kiss they had shared all those years ago.

Her fingers made their way to his chest, enjoying the way the hard planes of his muscles felt under her touch. She sighed against his lips as his hands moved away from her face and down her neck, drawing goosebumps along the way. A slight shiver fell from her body and made Garrett groan low.

His hands continued their journey down her body, stopping once they reached their intended destination: her breasts. Jules' soft whimpers grew louder as Garrett massaged her breasts. The sensations overwhelmed her senses, and they were only just getting started.

Their lips came apart, and he stared at her lips for a moment before he looked her in the eyes and said, "I want this off now, Jules."

His light southern drawl became more apparent when he was aroused, it seemed, and she loved the way he said her name. Without waiting for her to respond, he helped remove her shirt and quickly removed his own. He gently pushed her back onto the bed and the temporary pause in her movements gave her an opportunity to stare at the perfection that was his body once more. The evening she'd seen him shirtless when they'd first arrived at the safe house was only a small preview of the treat she was being given right now. She couldn't wait to get her hands on everything from his broad shoulders down to his chiseled abs. Her eyes traveled lower and saw that his dark denim jeans couldn't hide his readiness to take her.

Soon, his body was over hers, and he was back to kissing her lips as he slid her bra straps down her shoulders. He moved one bra cup out of the way and licked her nipple.

Jules closed her eyes and let out a low groan, enjoying the feel of his mouth on her. One palm found its way into his short brown hair, while the other clenched the bed sheets she was laying on. As he moved to uncover her other breast, she watched in awe before her eyes swung shut once more when he sucked on her nipple, while his hand continued to play with her other breast.

"Garrett," she said, breathlessly. That was the only thing her mind could think of outside of the pleasure he was bringing her.

"I love when you say my name. And I wish you could see the beautiful picture that I see, having you spread out in front of me like this."

Her eyes slid open, and she bit back a groan in annoyance when he moved off of the bed to take off his pants and boxer briefs. Jules balanced herself on her elbows, enjoying the mini strip tease she was getting as she watched him start to remove the rest of his clothes. His eyes never left her body as he stared at her while he tossed a condom that had been in his jeans on the bed.

"Someone was assuming that they were getting some tonight."

"I grabbed it after we got back here, in hopes that you would remember the kiss we shared. Thought I'd be prepared, just in case."

Thank goodness for that.

Any ideas about words that she could say in response flew out of her head as she admired the naked man in front of her. He didn't give her much warning before he was back on the bed, his body hovering over her own. He leaned down to give her another kiss before his fingertips expertly made their way down her body, toying with the waistband of her panties. It wasn't too long before he moved the last barrier out of the way, leaving her completely bare for his perusal. When he touched her again, she nearly buckled off the bed.

"You're ready for me." His comment ended with a moan.

She watched as he put on the condom and all she could do was nod. She held her breath in anticipation, and once he entered her, euphoria spread through her veins. As her body adjusted to his, she sighed in relief. This felt oh so right.

"Even better than I imagined," Garrett mumbled under his breath as he slowly moved inside of her.

Their connection was more intense than she could have ever imagined as she met his strokes. The pace that he had set was not doing enough for her because she wanted more. She wanted it all.

"Move faster, or I'm flipping us over and taking charge myself."

"Oh yeah?"

The dark edge to his voice told her that she might have made a mistake, but there was no way she was backing down now. "Yes."

And that was all it took. Soon, the couple was careening out of control and moving at a ferocious pace to take them both over the edge. The animalistic noise that left his mouth just as she found ecstasy told her that he was close. His tempo increased a tad before he grunted as he found his release. His eyes were closed as he was leaning over her, and when his eyes slowly opened and found hers, what she found in his both startled and warmed her soul.

17

Garrett sighed when his head hit the pillow, and once both of their breaths evened out from their extra-curricular activities Jules turned to him. "You look comfortable."

"Yeah, it's the first time I've laid in bed in quite a while."

"Was the couch uncomfortable?"

"I'm not going to deny that."

Jules sat up, pulling the sheet around her. "Then why didn't you say something?"

"Because I wanted you to sleep in here and get a decent rest, even if it meant that I didn't."

Jules stared at him, not quite sure what to say. His caring about her wellbeing, even if it meant that he ended up being uncomfortable, meant way more than she could put into words. "Thank you."

"Of course."

There was one thing she could give to him that would hopefully make whatever it was that they had going on better. "I want to talk about the night that everything happened."

Garrett stared at her for a beat before sitting up with his back against the headboard. He pulled Jules closer to him so that the two could cuddle while they had the discussion. Neither one of them knew where they would stand on the other end of this conversation, but it needed to be done.

"First, I want to apologize for everything. There are so many things that I could've done differently, and I wish I had."

"I have to accept part of the blame too, Garrett. I could have reacted differently, and instead I held a grudge against you for all these years."

Garrett rubbed his hand up and down Jules' arm. "You had every right to be pissed at me. I left you during one of your darkest times and when you needed me most. And the reason I did that was because I was a coward."

"What do you mean?"

"Around the time that you lost your grandparents, I found out I had gotten accepted into Knox. While we were friends that had slowly morphed into more, I knew I couldn't bring you down the road of what life might be like with me as I joined this organization. I wanted you to enjoy your life, discover new things, and I didn't want it to be that I was holding you back. So instead of telling you this in person, I left soon after I graduated. I know your grandparents died a couple of days after I left, but I didn't find out until months later. And by that point I knew you probably would want nothing to do with me, so I stayed away. Some of my assignments for Knox took me all over the world, but my thoughts never strayed too far from you. I'm so sorry."

As Jules digested the information, she almost felt as if she was reliving the pain and trauma that she'd dealt with all those years ago. One tear slid down her cheek as she said, "I was so angry at you for so long because I just knew you had to have known. The entire West family outside of you and Flint, who was deployed at the time, came to Grandma and Grandpa's funeral. I thought you were being an even bigger asshole for not showing up. Especially with how strong I thought our friendship had gotten while we were in college."

"I know. And I don't know if my parents mentioned anything, but they were also sworn to secrecy."

"That makes sense, I guess."

Garrett pulled Jules even tighter to decide. "When I did find out what happened, I was upset I couldn't have been there for you, and I knew that you got the worse of me. And I knew that it was well deserved."

"You know, being here with you unintentionally helped me deal with a lot of the hatred I had toward you. At first, I thought it was a result of us having to be a team while here, because essentially, we were almost cut off from everyone else that we know. But now I realize it helped shape how I could start the process of forgiving you. I won't say I'm completely there yet, and I understand that, at the time, we were very young and didn't know what the hell we were doing, but I'm happy I am on the road to getting there."

Garrett slowly nodded his head. "You know, I think that's the most open you've ever been with me. And I appreciate it."

"I think you're right."

She hoped she didn't end up regretting it.

"BREATHE."

Jules' eyes flew over to Garrett, preventing herself from giving her makeup in the vanity mirror in the car one more time. "I'm fine."

"No, you're not. I can feel the nervous energy flying all around you. I understand what you're feeling, but if you don't want anyone else to pick up on it, you're going to need to try to remain calm."

He was right, but she wasn't willing to admit that freely. This would be the first occasion she would be out in public since the threat on her life.

Things were still going well after the conversation the two had had a few nights ago. She was still living in the safe house with Garrett, enjoying the privacy of their own little bubble while they took their time getting to know each other once again. There were some moments where she felt as if they were back in college, enjoying the carefree nest of not having too many responsibilities due to being mostly away from the world.

But now they were back in the real world, for the time being.

They had just entered the fundraiser Jules had been scheduled to attend on behalf of the Cartwright Foundation. It would be no secret they were there together, although the two hadn't discussed what exactly they were to one another. Jules preferred to keep it that way, for fear of further complicating things.

Garrett stopped the car outside of the home of Ellis Washington, a board member for the Cartwright Foundation. The fact the event was taking place at his home was one of the reasons Jules had pushed so hard to go. She waited for the valet to come around and opened her door before stepping out of the car. Garrett took a moment to speak to the valet before he joined her, and together, they walked into the home.

"This place is stunning," Jules said.

"Yeah. No kidding."

The mansion was an off-white color with black roofing. Inside was designed with neutral colors as well and gave her an insight into what she imagined Ellis and his family were like outside of the work meetings she'd joined him on. The decor focused on more classic pieces, including a painting of what she assumed was one of their ancestors over the fireplace mantle, and kept the other things in the home more subtle. It was easily bigger than her parents' home and reminded her of something straight off the cover of an architecture magazine.

"I just wish we knew how to get to where the cocktail hour is..."

"May I help you, Miss?"

Jules turned around and found herself face-to-face with a smiling older woman.

"Yes, we were just trying to make our way toward where the cocktail hour is being held? My name is Jules Cartwright, and I am here on behalf of the Cartwright Foundation. My father should be here soon as well. He's sorry for being late."

"Oh, it's no worry at all. People will be coming and going the entire time. You're just gonna walk straight through those doors and head to the backyard. Everything is set up outside, including food and drinks. We have heaters, in case it gets chilly, as we assume it will as the day goes on, but Mrs. Washington was determined to have an event outdoors, so we did."

Jules giggled. "I can understand that. It is probably due to us only having a few more days of decently warm weather because we are getting deeper into fall."

"Don't I know it."

"Well, thank you for your help."

"It is my pleasure."

Jules and Garrett followed the woman's instructions and headed toward where they hoped was a backyard. As soon as they hit the patio, a server appeared in front of them with a tray carrying crystal stemware filled with mimosas.

"Drinks?"

"Absolutely, thank you very much," Jules said as she grabbed a mimosa.

The server turned to Garrett who just shook his head, indicating he didn't want to drink. The server soon turned away and headed for another group of people that had just arrived.

Garrett leaned down to Jules his ear. "I'm on duty."

She nodded and sipped from her drink, admiring the expansive backyard. It looked as if it went on for miles, and Jules wouldn't have been surprised if it did. She turned to look at Garrett, who was also surveying their new environment, but she suspected he was doing it for different reasons.

When he turned his attention back to her, she said, "I'm only drinking this to calm my nerves. It feels as if I haven't been around people, outside of you, in years."

"And wasn't it lovely?"

"It was." Jules took another drink, enjoying the sensation in her mouth. Maybe this wouldn't be so bad after all.

"But we also need to think about what happens after this is all done."

It took her a second to get the liquid down her throat, not expecting what had just come out of Garrett's mouth.

"Happens with what?"

"Us."

Before she could respond to what he had just said, everything seemed to go into slow motion as shots rang out.

18

J ules had been so startled by Garrett's words, that she'd turned her body toward him. She hadn't expected him to bring up their relationship or potential relationship so soon. Her crystal glass, which she'd had in front of her face moments before, shattered in her hand as the sound of gunfire filled the air. Garrett pulled her toward him, and he drove their bodies to the ground as they tried to find cover. More shots sounded, pinging the ground around them, but Jules couldn't tell where the shots were originating from as the other guests screamed and fled the yard. Panic drilled down in her chest, feeling like a heavy boulder laying on her body.

"Come on! Put your hands over your head and duck!"

Somehow Jules heard Garrett over all the hysteria that surrounded them from every angle and did as she was told. He immediately shielded her with his body the best way he could.

He rushed her through the house, and within seconds, she was thrown in the front seat of the SUV they'd arrived in.

It didn't take Garrett long to speed off down the street to a destination unknown.

"Are you okay?"

"Yeah, I'm fine."

"Are you sure?"

Jules nodded. "I have a small cut on my hand and need a change of clothes, but other than that, I'm fine." She glanced down at her now mimosa-stained dress before looking at her hand and noticing the slight shaking. She couldn't control the movement no matter how much she tried.

"I have a towel in the backseat and some tissues in the glove compartment." Garrett glanced at her, confirming what she said before he exclaimed, "What the fuck!"

Garrett's shout vibrated through the car. The scowl on his face and the crushing grip he had on the wheel was enough to turn her fear white hot.

How had she forgotten about the tissues? She quickly got a tissue for her hand and started blotting at the stain on her dress.

"Why did we leave there? It might have been safer to stay—"

"Jules, please, not right now." He glanced through the rearview mirror.

"But we might have been shot—"

"This vehicle is bulletproof, and there might have been a chance that the shooter could have come into the house and killed a bunch of people while trying to hunt you down."

"Are we sure the shots were aimed at me?"

"Based on where the shots landed? Yes."

He threw the words out there without sugarcoating it for

her, marking just how perilous the situation back there had become.

"I shouldn't have pushed us to go there. I put everyone's lives in jeopardy, and I'm so sorry."

Garrett turned to look at Jules, and she could see the fire burning in his eyes. If the same adrenaline was pumping through him as it was through her, she didn't know how he was able to focus on thinking straight, let alone driving. His eyes soon made their way back to the road before he pressed a button on the dashboard.

"Call Maverick and Axel."

Jules knew that Axel was in charge of her parents' security, so it made sense to call him too. As soon as the words left his mouth, the car followed directions and pulled the call together.

"Do not bring William to the event at Ellis Washington's home."

"Why? We're in the car on the way there now."

"There's been a shooting at the home."

Maverick cussed, and Axel must have had the call on speaker because Jules heard her mother scream in the background.

"Jules! Are you okay? Please tell me you aren't hurt!" The panic that filled her mother's voice filled her with dread. She didn't want to be the reason why her mother was filled with worry.

"I'm not, Mom. I might have a couple of small bruises, but I'm fine."

"We need to have a meeting, ASAP. This person is getting more brazen, and the sooner they are caught, the sooner we will all breathe a lot easier." Maverick's voice came through the speaker loud and clear.

Garrett nodded his head. "Let's meet at the Cartwright home immediately."

"I'm going to turn around as soon as I can and bring the Cartwrights back to their home."

"Excellent, Axel. What's your ETA, Garrett?"

Garrett answered Maverick's question immediately. "Twenty minutes."

"See you all soon."

The call ended just as quickly as it began, and Jules knew she was barely hanging on. Her hands were clasped together in her lap. She was almost afraid to let go, for fear that she might completely lose it. It didn't help that Garrett was also completely silent, allowing her to drown in her own thoughts about what had occurred just moments ago.

Her hands began to shake slightly as she tried to keep her composure, but knew she was failing.

WHEN GARRETT PULLED the car through the gates of Cartwright home, Jules felt more at ease than she had felt at home in a very long time. Gone were the stressors of always having to be perfect and in its place was a lot of vulnerability she had no problem wearing proudly. She had survived a suspected attempt on her life.

As soon as Jules crossed the threshold into her parents' home, she was wrapped up in her parents' arms, hugging as if they hadn't seen each other in years. William took a step back and allowed Carol to continue hugging their child.

When she finally broke the hug, Jules watched her mother take her time examining her, making sure what Jules had said on the phone was accurate.

"Oh, my sweet girl. You're staying here until this is all over. I don't want you out of my sight for the time being. What happened to your hand?"

"It's just a small cut, Mom."

"Let's get the first aid kit."

Jules thought it probably made more sense for her to stay at the safe house, because it lessened the likelihood of someone trying to enter her childhood home and harm her parents or someone on their staff. But who was she to deny her mother, especially if Knox had the home as secure as possible?

"That is something that can be discussed in the meeting."

Garrett looked at Maverick and said, "I'm going to nail this fucker to the wall."

William took a step forward and put his hand on Garrett's shoulder. "Let's get this meeting over with. I want this person off the streets before they harm my child again."

"I agree." Carol stood up and clapped her hands together once. "Let's get this meeting started so that everyone gets some rest."

"I don't know how much rest anyone will be getting anytime soon. I suspect that the police will eventually be making their way here," Garrett said.

Jules figured the same but hoped that her mother's thoughts would come to fruition first. The group followed William into the dining room where there was plenty of room for everyone to sit comfortably while Carol and Jules went upstairs. Carol helped Jules bandage her hand, and once

Jules changed her clothes, the two women headed back downstairs. In the dining room, Jules found a small arrangement of drinks and light refreshments and that the rest of the group had sat down and was waiting for the meeting to begin.

William cleared his throat as gestured with his hand to the three members of Team Knox. "Before we begin, I want to thank you, Garrett, for saving my daughter's life. If you hadn't been there, I don't want to think of what would have happened."

"Thankfully, we don't have to think about it."

William nodded, but said nothing more.

Maverick spoke next. "Staying here works since the infrastructure to protect Jules is already in place."

Maverick's comment caused a lot of nodding around the room.

"I agree." William looked at Maverick, Axel, and Garrett who were sitting next to one another. The men together looked as if it would take a crane to move either one of them before they would be able to harm anyone in this house.

"I contacted my son, and he said that he still has one of your men watching him, but nothing has happened to him, thankfully."

Jules bit her tongue before she asked if he actually called Sebastian. Granted, the situation probably called for throwing any drama that they had between each other to the back burner to find this person who was threatening their lives.

Jules sighed. "I'm glad he's not going through this."

Everyone turned to look at Jules, who was staring off into the distance out the window. She could feel that all eyes were on her, but she didn't acknowledge it.

"Although it's under bad circumstances, I'm glad you were able to come home for a bit."

Carol appeared next to her and laid her hand lightly on her daughter's back. She rubbed her hand up and down. The comforting gesture helped calm her nerves, which were still on edge from fleeing Ellis Washington's home.

"Thanks, Mom." Jules looked up at her mom briefly before turning her attention to the men in the room. "Dad, I know you didn't think Ellis had anything to do with this, but in the back of my mind, I couldn't help but think that his anger on the call he had with you could result in something like this happening. Now I'm not so sure. After all, now he is dealing with some of the damage that might have been caused by the gunshots."

"It could also be a way to shift suspicion away from him." Axel made a good point before drinking from his glass of water.

Maverick folded his arms over his broad chest. "I'm not ready to completely write him off, but I will say this moves him down the list of potential suspects."

Jules turned to look at Maverick. "Is there anyone else on the list?"

Before Maverick could respond, her eyes found Garrett's, but his expression gave nothing away. She quickly turned her attention back to Maverick.

"There are a few people that we've been looking into who might have a vendetta against your father. The issue is that it's harder to track their activities if they hired someone else to terrorize you, but we are trying our damnedest to find a connection. As of now, until we have more evidence pointing in a specific direction, the best thing we can do is keep you safe in case this person tries to strike again."

Jules nodded as she looked back at Garrett whose eyes were on her. She could feel her body start to heat up as his gaze caused a flame to burn deep inside of her. She wanted him to come over to her, sweep her into his arms, and take her upstairs to her old room and have his way with her. After all, it would take both of their minds off of the events that had occurred just a short time ago. Her thinking about doing this in her parents' home made her cheeks turn slightly pink, but their home was large, and her room was in another wing of the house from theirs.

The meeting continued and included a rundown of the latest information Knox had gathered and other measures that were being taken to keep the Cartwrights safe. When the meeting wrapped up, Jules started walking out of the room when she heard Garrett call her name.

She looked up to find him slowly walking toward her, his eyes displaying the unsureness that she felt. "Yes?"

Instead of stopping in front of her, he walked her over to a corner of the room where they wouldn't be overheard. "Are you okay? I noticed during the meeting that your eyes would glaze over every once in a while."

"Yeah, honestly, I think the adrenaline is wearing off, and I'm starting to get tired."

"Understandable."

She debated asking him the question that she had on the tip of her tongue, but she wasn't sure if she wanted to know the answer.

Garrett must have noticed the internal conflict she was

having with herself because he said, "What do you want to tell me?"

"It's more of what I want to ask, but I don't know if I want to know the answer." Admitting that felt as if she had ripped half of the Band-Aid off.

"Just ask it."

"What are we going to do about...whatever this is?" She gestured between the two of them with her hand.

Garrett didn't answer her question right away, instead choosing to stare into her eyes for a moment. She didn't know if he knew what he wanted to say, or if he was stalling while he came up with a response. Then he looked down at the floor before looking back up at her.

"I think we should keep things quiet between the two of us. I don't want Maverick to think I can't do my job because we are together, but that also doesn't mean I don't want to see you. I enjoyed our time together at the safe house."

Jules felt a little dejected at his response, but she also understood where he was coming from. "So, we should keep things strictly professional?"

"I didn't say that. I said we should keep things quieter. That doesn't mean I want to give up what we have, but all of the focus needs to be on finding the asshole who is trying to harm you."

"I understand that."

"Jules?"

Jules looked over Garrett's shoulder and found her mother standing there.

"Everything should be ready for you in your room, if you want to go upstairs and rest a bit."

Jules looked at Garrett briefly before giving him a small

smile and walking around him. She walked over to her mother, and her mother wrapped an arm around her as the two walked out into the hallway. Deep down, Jules couldn't help but wonder if things would be as simple as Garrett claimed once the culprit was caught.

19

"Checkmate."

Carol's sigh sounded almost comical as Jules moved her knight into place and declared checkmate. Jules couldn't help but feel good about meeting her mother in a game of chess. After all, it was she who first got Jules interested in the game.

Tonight was the evening after Jules moved back to her childhood home for the time being, and she and her mother had taken up the old pastime. Before Jules moved out and began living on her own, she would play a match with her mother at least once a week. It grew more and more infrequent until it stopped. Now, it felt good to get back to doing something that she remembered from childhood during a time like this.

The day after she had found herself running for her life, Jules would have taken anything that reminded her of happier times. The heart-pounding and stress she had experienced the day before had lessened, but she still found herself looking over her shoulder, even at her parents' home, where she knew, in the back of her mind, she was safe.

Jules stretched and stood up before turning to her mother.

"Is there anything I can get you?"

Carol looked at her daughter and shook her head with a smile on her face. "No, I'm just going to clean up and then probably turn in for the night."

"Are you sure I can't help you clean up?"

Carol looked at the chessboard. "I can handle this. Why don't you head upstairs and get some rest?"

Jules grabbed her phone and checked the time. She was shocked that it was almost ten P.M. She didn't know if it was her mom's question or her checking the time or maybe it was a combination of both, but she yawned, causing Carol to laugh. "I'll do that. I'll see you later, Mom."

Jules left the living room and walked toward the staircase that would lead toward her room. She glanced down the hall before walking up the stairs, wondering if Garrett was down there, sitting in one of the rooms that Knox had set up in her parents' home. Since they had gotten to her parents' house, she'd barely spent time alone with Garrett. She had seen him several times since yesterday, but they hadn't had a chance to speak, which she both understood and was disappointed by.

With a sigh, she reached her room and was happy it didn't take her long to prepare for bed, and once she turned out the lights, she hoped that sleep wouldn't take too long to come.

She was wrong.

Jules laid her in her childhood bedroom and tossed once more. She'd gone to bed hours ago but had never fallen asleep. Trying to get comfortable seemed to be a feat she couldn't reach as she stared up at the ceiling. Sleep wasn't coming anytime soon. Jules grabbed her phone and thought about scrolling through her social media site, but that wouldn't do anything but keep her up longer.

She scrolled through her text messages before she landed on the conversation she'd had with Garrett. She debated whether or not she should contact him. He and a few other Knox team members were staying in guest rooms in the Cartwright home, as well as the guesthouse that was on the property.

Jules put her phone face down. Messaging him would be foolish. The dynamic between them had changed with them being thrown into a new place and outside of the bubble that they'd formed being in the safe house together. She had seen him a few times during the last twenty-four hours, and the lingering looks he had given her told her that he was missing her just as much as she was missing him. So, what was stopping her from reaching out?

Throwing caution out the window, Jules picked her phone up and typed out a message.

Jules: Are you awake?

Garrett: Yes. Wrapping up a few things that I didn't have a chance to finish today. Why are you still awake?

Jules: Can't sleep.

She almost typed that she missed him but caught herself. She turned on the lamp on her bedside table just as Garrett sent another message.

Garrett: I could think of something that would help put you to sleep.

Jules refused to stop the grin that appeared on her face.

Jules: And what's that?

Garrett: I don't think you would have any issue figuring it out.

Jules: Doesn't mean that you couldn't spell it out for me.

Garrett: How about I give you something better? Make sure you leave your door unlocked because I have a surprise for you.

Jules didn't bother responding to his last message. Her heart pounded in anticipation and her desire for him began to build. When would he arrive?

Her question was answered soon after she asked as she heard the doorknob jiggle and the door slowly open. Jules sat up and watched as Garrett quietly walked into the room, with the stealth of someone half his size. Even while closing the door firmly behind him, his eyes never left her. She could feel the heat behind his gaze, searing her with thoughts of just how quickly it would take for him to cross the room and make her his. She would have thought that he would have dashed over to her bedside.

But he didn't.

Instead, he took his time, moving with precision, and causing her nerves to bubble under the surface. What was he going to do? And when was he going to do it?

Garrett still hadn't said anything as he studied her, taking her all in. Part of her wondered if he'd take his time looking around her room, where some of the nostalgia from her childhood remained, but he didn't. His eyes were completely focused on her.

"You're going to have to keep your voice low, you know that, right?" His voice was gruff, and Jules almost wondered if she'd heard him correctly.

"You haven't told me what we are doing, yet." She liked this small game of cat and mouse that they were playing. The fact they were in her parents' home raised her excitement more.

When he finally made his way to her, she stared up at him from where she was sitting on her bed. At any other time, this position would have meant that she was resting her body, but the tension that was strumming through her was allowing for anything but. He sat down next to her and brushed a piece of hair behind her ear, causing her to slightly tremble in response.

"What I'm going to do is going to have you begging for me to let you scream my name, but you're going to have to promise me that you won't. No one needs to know what we are doing, outside of you and me. Explaining this to your parents, even as an adult, would be interesting."

Jules chuckled. "I can do that. Keep quiet that is."

"Can you?" Garrett raised an eyebrow at her before his lips crashed into hers.

Her world exploded behind her closed eyes, and she relished the feel of his mouth being on hers. It felt as if it had been too long since they connected on this level, and she couldn't wait for more.

Garrett moved his head back slightly and said against her lips, "This might be a little quick. I need you now."

"I agree," she said. Happy the two of them were on the same page, she pushed her lips back toward his, and when his hands shifted her top out of the way and landed on her bare breast, she gasped, giving him the opportunity to slip his tongue into her mouth.

Their tongues danced a delicate dance with one another, tangoing as they battled for who would end up with the upper hand. Jules loved the game they were playing and smiled when Garrett pushed her back before he ended up on top of her. When he was taking off his shirt, she took a moment to let her hands dance over his chest, happy to be able to touch him again. Then his lips lowered to hers, and everything she was thinking fled her mind.

He was wearing a pair of dark colored cotton pajamas that did little to disguise his desire for her. She moved her hands down his body to touch him, and she felt him freeze under her touch.

"Jules, be careful."

She smiled briefly at his words, laced with warning. "I always am."

Garrett let her tease him for a few precious moments before it was clear he'd had enough. The stealth that he'd shown when he entered her room was nothing compared to the motions that he made to have her completely naked within seconds and underneath him.

"Just where I want you," he whispered before he was kissing her again, and his hands were roaming all over her body.

She was almost certain he had more than two hands at one point, because it seemed as if he was every at once, strumming her body to the beat of his own drum and making her grow closer to losing control. When his fingers landed where she wanted them to be since she'd sent that text message, Jules sighed in relief. But that quickly changed when he began to use his fingers to move against her, and she needed to cover her mouth to keep from squealing out loud.

"Good girl," he said as his motions picked up speed, and she lost it right there.

The look in his eye and the way he was making her feel

was driving her to the brink. And there was no way she would complain. Not now, not ever.

Without her saying a word about how close he was to getting her over the cliff, it was as if he sensed it, because he pulled away just before she could let go.

"What—"

"We're going together, sweetheart."

She felt him leave her briefly and heard the sound of a wrapper ripping in the distance. But it all didn't mean anything, because she was still soaking in the words that he had said. Something about them made her emotional, but she just chalked it up to everything that had happened over the last few days.

When he lined his body up with hers and then sank in, Jules couldn't stop from smiling. Garret smiled back at her in return, and without saying a word. It was as if they were communicating through their actions instead of dictating their thoughts with words.

When he began to move inside her, she bit her lip to keep from crying out in ecstasy. Their connection was the magic touch to righting everything that seemed wrong in her world at the moment and that made all of this worth it.

His body was so in-tune to hers that when she was close to losing all control, Garrett leaned down and kissed her, swallowing her cries of euphoria. When he joined her in her bliss, Jules rubbed his back slowly as they both caught their breaths.

When Garrett pulled her into his arms, she wondered how long things would stay like this. A connection that had developed as a result of being forced to stay together because of an unknown danger couldn't possibly survive once the danger was eliminated. Would this be one of the last moments that they spent together?

"Whatever you're thinking about so hard, stop. Everything will be fine."

Jules snorted, not caring how it sounded. "You don't know what I'm thinking about."

"I have a good idea, and I just want to tell you, not to worry about it."

WHEN JULES WOKE up the next morning, she was alone, but that wasn't surprising. She'd felt Garrett slip out in the middle of the night, she was supposed to keep what had happened between them a secret, and she didn't mind. The less she had to explain, the better.

Jules quickly took a shower and prepared for the day. With a light pep in her step that she could only attribute to the activities that happened the evening before, she walked downstairs to find out where everyone else in the house was.

It seemed as if her father and mother were busy doing their own things, so she decided to check up on Garrett in the room he was staying in on the other end of the house. After all, he'd come to her last night, and she was wondering if maybe another quick round would be on the cards for them. If not, it was completely understandable, seeing as how he was now back on duty.

When she reached the room where he was staying, she knocked on the door. She didn't get a response but could hear someone shuffling in the room so she knew he must have been in there. Maybe this would be an opportunity for her to sneak up on him.

Jules quietly opened the door and slid inside, closing it behind her. She crept as quietly as she could toward the doorway of what would have been a small attached sitting area of the room adjacent to the bedroom that Garrett was sleeping in. A quick sweep of the room before her eyes landed on his back told her that he turned it into a makeshift office.

"We could call Sebastian to see if his technical expertise could help us track him down. Might be helpful to have him on the ground here with his family, as well as working on any technical or hacking aspects right here."

Jules froze at the news but didn't make a sound. Had he just said what she thought he had just said?

"I know, but it's the only option we have right now. Plus, we know why Juliana is the target and not him."

It took everything in her to keep it together. What did he know, and when had he known about it?

She watched as Garrett ran a hand through his hair before he turned around. "It is something that we'll—"

Jules was standing directly in front of him with her arms folded. His eyes studied her, taking all of her in, and she knew there was no way that she was hiding any of the emotions on her face.

"Listen, I need to go. Something just came up."

With a decisive click, Garrett hung up the phone, and Jules was ready for battle. Checkmate.

20

"What are you keeping from me, Garrett?" Anger rated off of every word, letting him know that this wasn't a game.

"How much did you hear?"

"Enough to get what I think is a gist of what is going on here." The pieces started falling into place in her mind. "What do you mean that it might be better that Sebastian should be on the ground here? Does Sebastian work for Knox?"

Garrett didn't answer right away and that told her that her assumption was correct. When he nodded his head, she held back a scream.

"How could you keep something like this from me? How long has my brother been working for Knox? Is that why whoever this is, is coming after me and not him?"

"Now, Jules—"

"How could you do this again after everything we've been through?"

"Jules, it wasn't my place to tell you."

"Well, what can you tell me now? And how will I know that it is not a lie?"

"Come on, Jules, give me a break here. I didn't intend to lie to you."

"But you just did." She knew she sounded like a child, but she couldn't pretend to care. She was too hurt to care.

"I never wanted to hurt you. When Sebastian joined several years ago, he made me promise not to tell you, that he would tell you and your mother on his own terms. I didn't know that he hadn't told you all until your father asked that I help protect you."

One person's name was missing from all of this. "So, my father knows Sebastian is a member of Knox?"

Garrett rubbed a hand over his eyes, showing this wasn't a conversation that he wanted to have. "Yes, your father knows. As far as I know, he hasn't told your mother."

"If Dad knows about this, I have to assume then that he and Sebastian not getting along is a cover. So, all the excuses Sebastian's made about not coming home were a lie. It's because he was doing things for Knox." Everything was clicking into place.

"I can't confirm or deny that, but some of that needs to be taken up with your father."

"I'm sure my mom will have a lot to say about that as well, when she finds out." Jules let out a growl in frustration, but that wasn't the only thing that was released. The anger and tension she felt from being in this situation boiled over. "I thought we had worked this out. We were supposed to communicate and talk to one another."

She could tell her words stung based on the look on his face. He didn't say anything to refute her claims, either.

"We have been, and I—"

"Tell me this. Were you sworn to secrecy about my brother being a member of Knox? Or was this just Sebastian's doing?"

"Jules, I—"

"Tell me the truth!" Jules could tell he heard the pain in her voice based on the slight wince he made the louder her voice became.

"No, I wasn't. Once he was through training, which he has been for a while, it didn't need to be kept a secret. I'm sorry—"

Jules shook her head before she closed her eyes, trying to control her emotions. When she opened them again, she found Garrett standing closer to her, forcing her to look up at him from where she was standing. However, he was smart enough not to come too close, because she didn't know what she would do if he laid a finger on her.

"I'm pissed at him, but I'm more pissed at you. Because we just had a conversation about being open with one another the other day, and you failed to mention that my brother was a co-worker of yours? In a top-secret organization, none-theless. Could he have come home and protected me?"

"Sort of. He could have, but there was a slight risk he would be a target as well. Also, his cover would have been blown, because it's no secret to anyone you two aren't that close. His expertise is more in the realm of hacking, whereas I'm more qualified in this area."

"This is all too much," Jules said as she began to pace back and forth. She was grateful that Garrett didn't try to reach out and touch her, because she knew that would have further enraged her, and she needed time to think. "Mom is going to be so hurt. Here I was, worried about being the one who would cause her the most hurt, but who would have thought it would have been Sebastian. So maybe it is best that he comes back here and faces the consequences."

"Jules, can we talk about all of this? I can only imagine what is going through your mind."

"The time to talk about this has long passed. Unless there is something else you're keeping from me?"

She watched as Garrett took a deep breath and said, "We might have a lead on who is trying to kill you."

Jules' eyes widened but before she could say anything, Garrett put his hands up.

"This is a new development, and it hasn't been something I've been keeping from you. I just learned about it on that phone call."

"Please continue." The words that left her lips sounded harsher than she would have normally intended, but she couldn't care less.

"We believe it might be a family member of someone from your father's past. Someone he was in a relationship with."

"Oh, for the love of everything, please don't tell me that my father had an affair," Jules blurted out. She didn't know why she immediately jumped to that conclusion, but the way things were going and having the feeling that everyone she trusted was lying to her, it wasn't that far of a leap in her mind.

Garrett shook his head. "It was someone he dated before your mother."

A rush of relief flooded her body. At least her mother wouldn't have to deal with that. "Looks like another meeting needs to be held to disperse all of this information."

"One will be happening this evening when your parents are done with their obligations for the day."

Jules nodded, but the anger she was feeling toward him, toward Sebastian and her father was still there. She opened her mouth and quickly closed it. She did it again and sighed, willing the words that she wanted to say to come out. "I'm still angry at you, Garrett. Just because we've slept together doesn't give you the right to keep things from me!"

The door behind her clicked shut, and Jules spun around to see that they had an audience and her cheeks flamed. Her eyes went to Maverick's face and the pissed off glare he was giving her and Garrett.

"Tell me you aren't fucking our client's daughter, Garrett," he growled.

Garrett didn't say anything, but his expression turned unreadable.

"Dammit. You're trading places with Nash. I came in to tell you I have to go back to headquarters. I'll send Nash later, get your shit together."

"Wait, no—" Jules gasped.

Maverick just shook his head and left the room.

"Garrett, I—" She turned back around to see him shoving things in a duffle.

"I told you we had to keep this quiet," he muttered, sounding pissed off.

"But..."

"Just stop, Jules. There's nothing that can be done now. You'd better go."

Jules felt angry tears well in her eyes. Too much had just

occurred in a short span of time, and she felt overwhelmed by it all. She was angry and frustrated and she wanted to scream and yell about how unfair all of it was but knew that would just draw even more attention to them, so without another word, she stormed from the room, slamming the door behind her.

NEEDING to vent some of her anger, Jules went in search of her dad, wanting to confront him about Sebastian, but as she entered his study, her mother looked up at her.

"Sweetheart, is everything okay?" she asked softly, keeping her voice low as her husband was on the phone.

Jules stopped short and schooled her expression, pasting on the practiced smile she used at fundraisers. "Um, fine, Mom, just wondered where you and Dad were."

"We're just working on the West's college sponsorship plan that we're going to announce at the gala. Your father is on the phone with someone who wants to become a donor."

"Okay, do you need any help?" Jules felt like she needed to offer.

"Oh, no, we've got this, you just keep on with the gala, I know your father is determined that we still hold it as scheduled."

Jules nodded. "Okay." She turned and left, still feeling frustrated. As she headed back to her room, she pulled out her phone and called Sebastian.

"Jules, I'm a little busy at the moment—"

"How could you do this to me and Mom, Sebastian!" she

snarled into the phone, letting all her anger show in her voice.

"What are you talking about, Jules?"

"Knox!"

"You know?"

"How could you!"

"Does Mom know?"

"Not yet, but if you don't tell her, I will!"

"Look, I'm about to get on a plane, I swear I will tell her. I'll explain everything when I get there. Just, let me be the one to tell her, okay?"

Feeling only slightly better, Jules agreed. "Fine. But you better tell her soon. Have a safe flight."

"I will, Jules. Swear."

Jules hung up her phone, locked the door and sank down on her bed. She decided to throw herself into working on the gala. It was coming up and there was still a ton of work to do. She couldn't allow her personal life to spill over into her professional life.

About an hour later, a knock on the door drew her attention away from her laptop. She told the person on the other side of the door to come in. As the door opened, Jules adjusted the dark red sweater she had thrown on over her white tank top and navy denim jeans and looked over to see who was entering. She was somewhat surprised to find her mother, who looked to be upset.

"There will be a security meeting starting in a few minutes."

"Mom, is everything okay?"

"Sebastian called, told me that he's been working for Knox since he graduated. He was on the plane and only had a few minutes, but he wanted me to know before he arrived. Your father explained what he does, or at least what he knows. I just... I can't believe he kept this from me."

Jules looked down at her hands, standing up and walking over to hug her mother. She knew that being lied to had hurt her, but she could only imagine how her mother felt. "I'm so sorry, Mom. I, too, found out today."

"Your father mentioned it. I can't put into words how hard it is even to process this. I thought that they both would come to me with anything and then to have this thrown at me on top of the threats against you, I just..."

Jules tried to think back to when she'd seen her mother this upset before, and the only time she could think of was when her father's parents died. Over the years, Jules knew her mother had grown close to her husband's parents after losing her own when she was young so to lose them at the same time had rocked the entire family.

But even then, Carol had made an effort to appear strong, to not show weakness in front of the general public. From what Jules could remember, she even made sure not to cry in front of her immediate family members, determined to be the rock everyone needed in their time of need. That was where Jules had gotten it from, but now the tables had been flipped, and Jules knew she needed to be there for her mother.

Jules pulled back and swept the wisps of hair that had crowded her mother's face away. She took her time fixing her mother's hair and then moved to grab a tissue from her desk and wipe her tears away. They were both going to go into the meeting with their heads held high, no matter what further information was thrown at them.

"I'm not upset that Sebastian works for Knox. I'm upset that both he and your father felt the need to keep it from me."

"I know, Mom," Jules said as she pulled her mother back into her arms. She felt similarly, although she recognized that her mother probably felt worse. All this time that Sebastian hadn't been around had hurt her mother. Who knew what tales her mom had spun in her head about why her only son didn't come home to visit her more frequently, and it turned out to be because of this.

"We are going to go down there, and whatever happens, happens. None of this hiding our feelings anymore, or any more secrets. We deserve to let our feelings be known, especially after our ability to voice our opinions was taken away from us."

Carol nodded her head and gave her daughter a sad smile. "I'm so happy that you grew up to be so wise."

Jules shrugged. "Honestly, this all kind of fell into my lap over the course of this whole debacle. It forced me to realize things that I hadn't paid much attention to before. And for that, I'm glad."

21

J ules walked into the living room with her mother, holding her hand as she led her to the couch. She looked both at her father and Garrett as she sat down, not afraid of what she would find coming from either man. Her father's sights were set on his wife, and as soon as both of the women in his life were seated, he walked over to greet them and pulled up a chair next to his wife. He whispered something in her ear that Jules didn't catch before grasping her hand and putting it into his lap.

When Jules' attention shifted to Garrett, she found him staring at her in a way that was almost unnerving. She'd gotten used to the way he looked at her, but this was different. The situation was different.

His gaze carried a lot of things she wasn't expecting. Hurt and pain registered first before he turned his attention to the screen where Maverick's head just popped up. Her eyes lingered on him for a few seconds longer, as regret for what happened earlier that day appeared in her mind.

It seemed as if Maverick would be joining them from a

remote location and they needed to stream his feed onto the big screen television in the living room.

"Good evening, team. I hope everything has been quiet there, which would be good news."

If he only knew.

"The first update I have is that Nash will be coming in to switch places with Garrett tonight, while Garrett is reassigned to another location."

Jules once again regretted arguing with Garrett, not because it wasn't a legitimate argument, but because it led to him being pulled from her detail. She was still mad at him for keeping things from her, but she'd never intended to get him sent away. Her eyes shot over to Garrett, who refused to look anywhere but at Maverick who was still speaking to the room.

She could see that her father was about to speak when Maverick paused but swallowed his words when he looked at Jules.

"Since no one has anything to say about that, I would also like to add that in addition to Nash joining, Sebastian will be en route as well."

It seemed as if Maverick had no issues talking about Sebastian freely now that everyone in the room knew the secret that had been kept for several years now. With all that being said, at least her brother was coming home even if he had a lot of explaining to do.

"Now let's talk about what intelligence we've gathered recently. William, did you know a Marie Warner?"

William thought for a moment. "Yes. We dated briefly in my twenties. Why?"

"She recently passed away."

The whole room sat there in silence, taking in the news. Although her father was the only one who knew anything about her personally, there was a moment of silence to mourn the loss of life.

"The only family she had left was a nephew who was her caregiver until the end."

"What does all of this have to do with the threats against Jules?"

Jules was happy that her father spoke up again because she was wondering the same thing.

"It seems as if he blames you for everything that went wrong in Marie's life. At least, according to the social media posts he's made over the last few months or so."

Maverick's face left the screen and what replaced it was screenshots of posts from several social media sites, all from the same person, stating how he hated William Cartwright and how his children would pay for the sins of their father. The screen shifted back to Maverick.

Although she wanted to give her father the benefit of the doubt, after everything that happened over the last twenty-four hours, Jules felt as if the question must have been asked. "Dad, what is all of this? Are you sure nothing else happened between you and Marie?"

"I swear on everything that nothing else happened between me and Marie. We ended things amicably, and I met your mother a few months later. We've, of course, been together ever since. What story her nephew has spun up, I have no idea. I haven't been in contact with Marie in years."

"How long ago is 'years'?" This time, it was Maverick asking the question.

"Um, after both Sebastian and Jules were born. She'd

come to me when she was having some money troubles, and I gave her some money to tide her over until she landed on her feet. Maybe a few thousand? I'd have to go back and look through my records. Anyway, after I sent her the money, that was the last I heard from her, so I assumed she was living comfortably."

Carol nodded in agreement. "Was this the old friend you told me that you were helping out of a tight spot?"

William nodded. "Yes, it was her."

"I vaguely remember that happening because I believe that he mentioned it off hand when we were chatting, just before Jules' ballet recital began." Carol smiled at the memory before she turned back to Maverick.

Garrett cleared his throat and took a step forward. Jules couldn't help but to look at him, standing there, looking as if he owned the room. Gone were any signs of hurt and pain he had shown earlier and in its place was strength and the desire to take charge of moving the ship back on course. "What do we know about the nephew? Where is he now?"

"I'm glad that you asked," said Maverick with a smirk on his face. "His name is Jesse Warner, and here is a photo of him."

When a picture of the man appeared on the screen, the first thing Jules thought was she had never met this man before in her life. The photo looked dated and there was something vaguely familiar about him, but she could chalk that up to him not having any distinguishable features. "I don't think I've ever seen him before."

William chimed in, "Me either, but that's not saying much. I see so many people regularly that I might have and just don't remember it."

Maverick continued, "This photo is several years old, so we don't have much to go on in terms of what he looks like now. Outside of the social media posts that we were able to track down to a library near where Marie lived, he's pretty much been off the grid. We do have trackers on him in case he uses any of the electronics or credit cards we believe he has access to."

William turned to look at Jules before looking back at Maverick. "So, the only suggestion you have is we should wait?"

"Unfortunately, yes. We have some of our people hunting him down, but there's little we can do until he resurfaces. All we can do is remain vigilant and wait him out. If he's as angry as his posts indicate he is, he'll reappear and when he does, we'll get him."

"Wait," Jules said. "Do we know if he knows how to shoot a gun?"

She could feel Garrett's eyes on her as she made a reference to the event that they had attended together just a few days ago.

"He's been known to go to the shooting range, according to some older posts, so him knowing how to shoot a gun wouldn't be a surprise."

So, there was a good chance he had been the one to fire at her. But if he was trained in shooting, why had he missed? Was his only objective to send a warning to her? A shiver ran down her spine as she realized he might have been way closer to her than she'd originally thought.

22

"What do you mean Garrett left?"

The shock evident in Liv's words translated through the phone with no issue and showcased exactly how Jules felt. She couldn't believe he'd done it either, but she couldn't blame him after the way she'd acted.

"He did. I thought he would have just moved to another post here, but no. Nash is my new bodyguard until Jesse is caught. I still can't believe Maverick moved him away, I thought maybe he'd just be moved off my detail, but he's got to go back to headquarters. I know he said we had to keep what was going on between us, but I didn't know this was why—"

Liv scoffed. "You know, you could have still spoken up. Said you wanted him to stay on location, even if he wouldn't be on your detail. He did save your life, Jules."

Jules didn't say anything because she knew that her friend was right, so Liv continued.

"Just wow. Everything that you've told me wouldn't have

made me think that either of you would have given up so easily."

"I know, but I think I was just too angry at the time to speak up and then at the meeting I just didn't know what to say to fix it without making things worse. I'm still mad at him. He shouldn't be keeping things from me if we're going to be together."

"I don't blame you for snapping at him, I mean keeping the fact that your brother works for Knox a secret, well. We now know what kind of danger they get into. I'd be pissed if someone in my family kept that kind of secret from me, even if they are supposed to be a kind of secret agency. It's family."

Jules sighed and rubbed her hands down her face. She still felt hurt over what she felt was deceit on his part, but he was right. It wasn't his information to tell. But it brought back memories of what he had done just before her grandparents passed away, and the pain that she thought she'd done a good job of moving on from was still there barely under the surface.

"Liv, it's just complicated, and I don't know how to proceed with any of this." Jules ran her hand through her hair for the fiftieth time but couldn't care less about how messy it looked.

"Talk to him? The only way he's going to know how you feel is if you talk to him."

Jules pulled the phone away from her ear and stared at it. "Since when did you get so good at giving advice?"

"I won't take offense to what you said, and I have my moments."

Jules chuckled before she sobered up. "I really need to

make this right, and I can't have this weighing on my conscience."

"You like him a lot, huh?"

Jules' grin could not be contained. "I guess I do. Haven't had to admit that out loud before."

"Happy to be the first to hear it. I need to head back into this wedding and make sure everything is still running smoothly. I just wanted to call and check in."

"Okay, I'll talk to you soon." Jules hung up the phone and looked around her room. What else could she do to amuse herself for a few hours? It was too early to play chess with her mother, and she knew her father's schedule was jam packed with back-to-back meetings.

Before she could think of anything else, her phone buzzed. She hoped it was Garrett messaging her but was shocked yet disappointed by the message she found.

Sebastian: Jules, I know you're pissed at me, but I wanted to let you know I'll be home soon, and I hope you'll allow me to explain everything.

Jules: I hope you plan on speaking to Mom first. She's very upset about all of this.

Sebastian: I am. I talked to her before I left and told her my plans.

That answer satisfied Jules. After all, one of her main goals was to make sure that her mom didn't worry more than she had to at any given moment.

Jules: Sounds good. I'll see you when you get here.

Her short message with her brother was enough to distract her temporarily, but she needed to find something else to do. The urge to send a text message to Garrett was still there, but she refrained. She needed to think of exactly what she wanted to say to him in order to avoid saying something she might regret.

Jules put her phone in her pocket and set off to grab a snack from the kitchen. After gathering some crackers and cheese and filling a water bottle that she received in college, she almost ran headfirst into Nash.

"Everything okay?"

Jules nodded. "Just grabbing something to eat."

This was pretty much how her interactions with Nash had been since he arrived. Whenever they ran into each other, he would make sure everything was okay before returning to do whatever he was doing. While she had no ill will toward the man and thought he was doing a good job, he wasn't Garrett. In her eyes, she knew no man would ever measure up to him in terms of keeping her safe. Maybe her father was right and that he did hire the best man for the job.

She sighed, her phone in her pocket feeling even heavier than before. She knew she had to contact him, and she wished the words were easier to come by. As she took the snacks and drink back to her room, the words she wanted to tell Garrett began to form in her head, creating the picture she wanted to paint in her mind.

Once she was settled back at her desk, Jules took her phone out and stared at it. Her thumbs hovered over the screen wondering where to begin with the words that threatened to flow from her fingertips.

Jules: Hey. I'm sorry I didn't listen to you and keep quiet about us being together. I shouldn't have eavesdropped on your conversation, and I shouldn't have reacted the way I did. I never intended to get you pulled from my detail. I was hurt and trying to protect myself.

Before she could doubt herself, Jules pressed send, checked the time and put her phone down on the table. She finished up the food that she had eaten and checked her phone to see if Garrett responded. She was disappointed to find nothing there.

"Calm down. You only sent the message a couple of seconds ago," she mumbled to herself as she gathered the dish that she used.

Jules checked her phone one more time before laying it back down on her desk. She left her room with the dish, planning on taking it downstairs to wash off so that it wouldn't get in the way of Patricia making dinner.

It seemed as if no one was near the kitchen or the living room when she walked down there. She took her time cleaning the dish and setting it in the drying rack, deeming that it wasn't even worth placing it in the dishwasher since it was only one dish. She was just about to dry her hands off on a nearby dish towel when she heard another voice in the room.

"Jules?"

Jules nearly jumped out of her skin at the new voice in the room. She turned and found Patricia standing behind her. She was happy it was the woman who had helped keep the Cartwright household running for years and not someone else, but she couldn't deny that she wasn't startled. "You almost gave me a heart attack."

"I'm sorry. I walked in and saw you were washing something, and I was going to tell you not to worry about it."

Jules shrugged. "No need. I didn't want to make any more work for you."

Patricia waved her off. "Nonsense. I was just about to get

ready to start cooking, and it would have been no trouble at all."

Jules smiled. "Do you need any help with anything?"

"Nope. Everything is good here. I'll call everyone down when dinner is ready."

Jules nodded and turned on her heel to walk into the hallway and back up the stairs to her room. When she reached her desk, she held her breath hoping that when she lifted her phone, she would find the notification she was looking for.

But there was nothing.

Frustration grew to a point that she couldn't quite control, and she knew she needed to take a breather. She grabbed a coat that she'd tossed over her chair and threw it on. Since she knew her childhood home better than anyone, it didn't take her long to find an exit that hadn't been completely secured by Knox and make her way outside.

Deep down, she knew she should have alerted Nash to her whereabouts but talking to anyone else right now about anything would just fuel the fire burning inside of her. She knew she shouldn't be upset, but she was hoping to be on the road to patching things up with Garrett sooner rather than later...if he forgave her overaction.

Jules jumped when she heard a loud bang behind her.

"What the—"

But her words were cut off. For a flash of a second, she saw at least one man dressed in all black. Before she could react, someone grabbed her from behind.

"No!" she screamed, just before a hand slammed down over her face. The pain from the impact rocked her mind in a way she couldn't describe, causing her to become disoriented.

Jules thought she might have heard someone else yell, but she couldn't tell if it was real or her imagination.

Jules tried to scream again even if her mouth was covered, in hopes that any sound would alert the security that had been hired to protect her.

The person who was holding her said something, but their words were muffled. She assumed the person had a mask on. Within seconds, something was thrown over her head, surrounding her in darkness that she feared that she would never get out of. By the time her body hit the cushion of what she assumed was some sort of vehicle based on the cool leather under her fingertips, she allowed herself to succumb to her body's desire to pass out.

23

Jules could feel herself coming to, but she was afraid to wake up. Afraid of what might wait for her on the other side of consciousness.

The events that had taken place earlier that evening flooded her mind as she fought the desire to wake up. Maybe if she pretended that what she experienced wasn't happening then she could fall back to sleep. She knew it was a coping mechanism that wouldn't serve her well in the long term, but any other option right now terrified her.

"Wake up."

The voice came from somewhere to her left she thought... or was it her right? Jules had no idea what to think, other than she was laying on her side on a hard surface. She debated opening her eyes and hoped the man who said those words couldn't see that she had. Then again, how did she know he was the only one in the room?

Gathering enough courage, Jules cracked open one eye and tried to get her bearings before the man who was in the same room as her, realized she was awake.

She found herself in a dimly lit room that resembled a living room. It looked as if it had seen better days based on what looked to be a worn-out rug and rips in the couch. Where she was though, she had no idea, but at least from where she was, there was no one standing in front of her.

"I said, wake up."

The voice sounded more aggravated than before, causing Jules to force her eyes open. She didn't want to piss whoever this was off more than he was already.

Jules moved her body slightly, testing out what kind of state it was in. Did she have any bruises? Broken bones? Anything that might hinder her from breaking away when the time came for her to do so. As she stretched her body out, she didn't think anything was broken, which was a breath of fresh air to her cloudy mind. She didn't know how sturdy she was on her feet yet, but at least this was something.

The next thing Jules noticed was that she wasn't tied up or down to anything. What kind of kidnapping was this? It didn't make any sense to allow her to have this much freedom.

She slowly brought herself into a sitting position and got a better idea of the room around her. It was definitely lived in, but the thick layers of dust everywhere told her it had been a long time since it had seen a deep cleaning. She licked her chapped lips before slowly turning her body to face what she assumed would be the man who had spoken to her.

When she came face to face with the only other person in the room, she gasped. "It's you."

The smirk that appeared on his face was sinister in nature. "It's me," he said mockingly.

The man she had seen her father talking to at the fundraiser weeks ago was sitting down in a dark brown chair a few feet away from her. She'd known the photo that Maverick had shown during one of their meetings had looked familiar, but she couldn't place him. Now everything started to click into place.

"You were speaking to my father at the South fundraiser." He was the man who William tried to end the conversation with but couldn't until Garrett and his father had showed up.

"Right again. You're pretty good at this."

"But why? What's the point in kidnapping me? Going through all of this trouble to do...all of this?"

Jules chose her words carefully on purpose as not to upset Jesse. She didn't want to anger the man who might have the ability to hurt her.

"Because it's time for your father to pay for what he has done."

"What did he do? I heard that your aunt died, and I'm sorry that that happened to you. I know what it's like to lose someone you're close to."

Jesse scoffed. "I lost her long before she finally left this earth. All thanks to the almighty William Cartwright."

His words confused her based on what her father had told everyone, and Jesse was now telling her. "I'm confused. Please explain."

Jules hoped her ability to remain expressionless, and her appeal to connect with Jesse would end up saving her life. She knew he knew how to shoot a gun, even if she couldn't see it. She didn't want to take the chance that he had it nearby and would use it on her.

She took the opportunity to glance around the room and tried to plot a way to escape. Jules thought she could try to run past him and into what she thought might be a hallway, but there was no guarantee what was waiting for her there. Jules assumed Jesse had to have someone else when he came to kidnap her so where was that other person? In addition to that, she needed to get around him in order to make it there and given she didn't know how sturdy she was on her feet, it might not be a good option for her either.

Jules tried to look to see if any of the windows that were behind her might be a good escape route. Her thoughts swirled around. It looked to be dark outside, and she didn't know if that would hurt or help her, but she was soon startled when Jesse moved.

He stood up and began to walk back and forth. "Aunt Marie lost everything about twenty years ago. I know she was at her wits end and felt as if she didn't have many choices. So, she went to your father and asked for money, and he told her to get out of his office."

How hadn't he noticed that she was trying to figure out a way to get out of here? She wasn't exactly being inconspicuous while looking around the room. "I'm sure there must have been some misunderstanding." Jules didn't want to be combative toward him, but she believed her father's words over his.

Jesse vehemently shook his head before he looked at her. His eyes stared through her, and she wondered if her ability to act indifferent was actually working or just further pissing him off. When he started walking again, she breathed a sigh of relief. It was clear she hadn't pissed him off enough for him to hurt her. "And we're going to clear this 'misunderstanding' right up."

Jules' thoughts spun as she tried to figure out what he could possibly mean by that. Those thoughts stopped when she heard a faint knock on the door. "What's that?"

A subtle smile once again appeared on Jesse's face. "You'll know soon enough."

Jules swallowed hard as she watched him walk out of the room without another word, and her confusion increased. She positioned her hands so that she could push herself. She didn't know how much time she had, and she needed to move as soon as possible. The fact that she wasn't restrained or locked somewhere was a gift, and she shouldn't waste this opportunity.

As she pushed herself into an upright position, Jules tested her ability to stand, and while she felt a little wobbly, for the most part she felt okay, which was another positive in her book. She couldn't go in the direction he'd just walked in which meant the hallway and front door were out. She tiptoed over to the living room window and moved the large curtains that covered them. When she tried to pull the window up, she noticed that the windows had locks on them, creating another barrier for her to get through if she wanted to get out of here.

"Shit," she mumbled to herself as she turned back around. Jules assumed Jesse would be back in the room at any minute so she sat back down on the floor where she had been before, hoping he wouldn't notice she wasn't in the exact same spot that she had been in before. As soon as Jules had sorted herself once again on the floor, Jesse rushed back into the room.

"I have a surprise for you."

Jules' heart leapt into her throat as she waited to see what he would bring into the room. The shock that registered on her face when her father entered the room couldn't be moved no matter how much she tried. The mask she'd kept on while trying to sort through this mayhem slipped when she saw his face.

"Dad!" she exclaimed just before her father pulled her into his arms. He hugged her tighter than she could ever remember him doing so, and when he pulled back, she asked, "How did you find me?"

"It's a long story, but I'm just so happy you're okay. It's been hours since we've heard anything from you."

Jules did a double take. "I've only been here an hour."

William shook his head. "No, it's been more like three or four. Jesse here contacted me and said that if me and your mother wanted you back alive, I needed to come to Marie's house alone. So here I am."

That connected a few more dots for her as her father pulled her behind him, sticking his body between her and Jesse. She also figured that if her father was here, then Knox must have a plan as well to see that this comes to an end tonight.

William turned to Jesse and said, "Now that I've done as you've requested, it's time that you let her go. You got what you wanted and that's me in the room with you."

Jesse glared at William and said, "You don't get to make the demands here. Whatever I say goes."

Jules glanced up at her father before turning her attention back to Jesse. She saw that her father had turned slightly red, indicating he was getting angrier by the minute. She knew she needed to defuse the situation immediately. "Dad,

Jesse's been a very gracious host, and I think it's better if we listen to him, okay?"

William looked behind him and raised an eyebrow at his child before looking back at Jesse. She figured he probably thought she must have some sort of injury due to her not being able to recall how long she'd been missing and the words that had just come out of her mouth. However, she had worked too hard to get on Jesse's good side to have it ruined, just in case it meant saving both of their lives.

Jules cleared her throat. "Jesse, now that you have my father here, could you tell him about the misunderstanding? Maybe we can fix this right now."

Instead of doing as she asked, Jesse turned and slammed his hand against the wall, causing her to jump and for her father to further push her behind him. "William here knows what he's done. He left my aunt in dire straits because he'd moved on and had his perfect family."

Jules cast a sideways glance at her father and watched him slightly turn pale. What didn't she know about this situation?

"When Marie came to me asking for help to get her out of a tight spot, I did what I could to help her and that was the last time I heard from her."

"Liar." Jesse's voice was barely a whisper, which made the word sound even more scary. That was until he whipped a gun out from his waistband and pointed it at William. "You never gave her anything and left her when she couldn't give you what you wanted: an heir."

Jules stood rigidly behind her father scared to even take a breath in case that led to her death. She couldn't believe her ears. There was no way this was true, was it?

Her father's hand tightened around her hand, and he squeezed her hand twice. What she didn't know was that it was a sign until she looked up.

24

Jules could have cried tears of joy when she saw Garrett standing before them, his gun drawn and pointed at Jesse. She hadn't been expecting Garrett to come, and her heart almost sang. How his entrance here was completely different from the reaction she had when he walked into the Green Hat with Rae and Flint, which now seemed like forever ago. Garrett's eyes never left his target, and while she had been relieved to see her father appear before her, she felt safer now that Garrett was in here. Maybe they would make it out of this alive.

"Nice of you to join us, Garrett West. Couldn't let us have all of the fun, could you?"

"Jesse, this doesn't have to end this way. Put the gun down, I'm warning you." Garrett shifted his body and took big steps to walk around Jesse and head over to where Jules and William stood. When he paused, he was standing in front of Jules and her father, and it was clear he hoped to protect them in case Jesse fired a shot. That was helpful as she watched Jesse tighten his grip on the gun. His finger hovered along the barrel, and she wondered if he would pull the trigger, causing a whole different series of events to occur.

"Oh yeah?" Jesse sent Garrett a cocky look but didn't move his gun an inch. "What are you going to do? Shoot me? I'm as good as dead now anyway."

Fear made Jules gulp as the blood in her veins turned to ice. Having someone point a gun at her was one thing but knowing that that person thought they had no other choice, nor that they didn't care what happened to them was an entirely different matter and was extremely frightening. If she had to bet money on it, Jesse knew there was a chance he wasn't going to make it out alive, and he didn't care.

"Put. The. Gun. Down."

Jesse smirked in response, instead tightening his grip on his weapon. It was almost as if Garrett hadn't said a word at all. Jules' eyes darted between the two men and the difference between them was staggering. Garrett looked to have the utmost confidence while Jesse had a slight shake in his stance. She, of course, had more confidence in Garrett's ability to handle the situation, but also understood that Jesse was a wild card here, and there was no telling what he would do.

William coughed lightly. "The reason why Marie and I broke up had nothing to do with her ability to have children."

Although no one shifted their guns or their stances, Jules noticed the attention had shifted to her father as the room waited for him to continue.

"We separated because she thought being under the microscope that would have been my world, wasn't a life she wanted to have. So, we amicably separated. I heard from her every so often throughout the years and we would chat maybe once every few years. When she asked me to help her out of a tough situation she was in, I did, and that was the last time I heard from her until someone told me about her passing. And that's the truth."

Jules could see that her father had adjusted his approach to Jesse, instead speaking softer versus the anger that had been in his voice when he walked into the room. Jesse's body shook slightly before his head followed suit. "That's not true. You ruined her life."

"Who told you that?"

"She did. Look, she was all I had left after my mother died, and when I came to her, I saw the condition she was in. Hell, you can see it just by looking around this home. So, I spent the last few years of my life trying to fix this place up and make sure that we had enough money to survive on as well as be able to afford the medical help she needed."

William shook his head. "I told her I wouldn't say anything about this to anyone because she didn't want to discuss it, but I gave her money to help pay for medical bills that included helping her fight an early-onset Alzheimer's diagnosis. I didn't visit because she didn't want me to see her that way, but I'm sure as her caregiver, you noticed changes in her over the months and years."

It was clear William had struck a chord because Jesse's eyes shifted, and he lowered the gun slightly. "But she said you did. And when she did say it, she meant it because those were the days that she remembered who I was."

"We were able to confirm William's version of events and find that Marie did, in fact, cash a check from him. We are happy to show you the banking records we managed to pull, but she might have even kept the check. Jesse, we know how much of your life you gave up taking care of your aunt, but this doesn't need to be the end. You have so much of your life to live. Don't give it up now because of this."

Garrett seemed to take on the same tone Jules and William had before him, and his words seemed to have the most effect on Jesse. Jesse's eyes darted around the room, looking at every person nervously. Garrett still hadn't adjusted his stance, and Jules knew he was ready to pounce if warranted. She could see tears welling up in Jesse's eyes before his lips began to quiver.

"Jesse, I know you don't want to do this. Just put the gun down, and we can figure out a way out of this. I think I can say you and William would both agree Marie wouldn't have wanted you going down this road."

Jesse nodded as the tears freely fell down his face. He lowered the gun to his side with his eyes on the ground, and Garrett walked up next to him and snatched the gun out of his hand. As Garrett was checking to make sure Jesse didn't have any more weapons on him, William pulled his daughter into his arms and gave her a big hug. The two didn't say anything as more people started to enter the room.

Jules and William broke apart, and Jules found herself face to face with Garrett.

"Knox agents are here to get everything squared away."

Jules took a step back from her father and flung herself at Garrett. "I didn't know if I'd ever see you again."

Garrett pulled her into his arms and gave her a tight, warm hug. "There was no way that that would have happened. I wouldn't have let it."

"There's so much that we need to talk about."

She could feel him pull apart from her slightly and she looked up into his eyes.

"We can do all of that later. Once everything settles down."

Jules nodded and pulled Garrett into another hug. Nothing else mattered because she was back in his arms. Except when there was a slight cough behind them.

They pulled apart and looked at William who had a small smile on his lips. "Is there something that you want to tell me?"

25

Jules watched as Knox employees filed in and out of Marie and Jesse's home, gathering evidence and cleaning up things that were left lying around. Although there had been a lot of commotion, it was fortunate that there had been no shots fired because it made things easier for them to do their job. Or so Garrett said. There was so much she had to learn about Knox.

Standing outside of the home where she'd been held captive for well over a day was a surreal experience. She watched as Jesse was led out in handcuffs. He glanced at them as he was escorted to a large, dark-colored SUV.

"Wait," Jules said as she walked closer to the SUV. "There's one more thing I would like the answer to."

Jesse just stared at her, not giving away whether he would respond to her request.

"What was the point of the birthday card?"

"It was symbolic. I sent it to you because Marie wouldn't have any more birthdays." Jesse turned toward the driver's seat. "I'm ready to go now."

The driver of the SUV pulled Jesse's window up, effectively cutting off the conversation and Jules took a step back before the SUV pulled away.

She snuggled deeper into Garrett's black hoodie that he'd given her just before they walked outside, and she said, "You know what?"

Garrett and William looked over at her, before William responded, "No, what?"

"I wonder how much Jesse actually wanted to hurt any of us."

"What makes you say that?" This time it was Garrett who spoke.

"Yes, he had a gun, but he didn't point it at me until Dad came into the room. He also could have easily shot and killed me at Ellis Washington's home if he had wanted to, based on the training we think he has, but he didn't. He also never tied me up and allowed my dad to just waltz into his place, which I'm not sure how you found me anyway."

"Garrett thought the first place we should look was here, and it turned out that he was right." Jules looked up at Garrett and gave him a smile before William continued. "I offered to go in there unarmed because I knew the person he actually wanted was me. Garrett said he would give me a couple of minutes to talk Jesse into surrendering and if I hadn't, he was coming in."

"Jules! William!"

Everyone turned around and saw Carol running toward them. But she wasn't alone. Sebastian was jogging alongside her. A heavy sigh of relief left Jules' lungs, when she saw the rest of her immediate family coming toward them. It was over. Finally over.

Her mother quickly pulled Jules into her arms and squeezed her so tightly that Jules didn't know if she would ever let go. No one said a word and Jules was fine with that. No one else knew the feelings she was trying to process due to what had happened over the last several hours, and Jules loved being back in her mother's embrace.

"You don't even want to know the thoughts I was having, and then when your father offered to go in, I..."

Jules nodded. "Mom, we don't ever have to speak about it because I'm fine. Everyone is fine."

Even in the dim light, Jules could see the tears forming in her mother's eyes. Carol must have noticed the tears at the same time because she did her best to wipe them away, before turning to her husband. "I'm so happy you're safe. And thank you. You helped to save our child."

William pulled his wife into his arms just as Jules turned around to face the other person that joined the party. "Sebastian."

It had been months since she'd seen her older brother. His normally shorter hair was longer and curlier than she was used to. It reminded her of some of the photos her mother had in the house of Sebastian when he was a toddler, only his hair was darker now.

"You have a lot of explaining to do," Jules said. She wasn't mad about the situation anymore, more so disappointed.

"I know. And I promise to tell everything."

She gave her brother a small smile before he gave her a hug. "I'm just glad you're okay."

"Good work, Garrett."

Jules and Sebastian pulled away from one another, and

everyone turned around and found Maverick standing behind them.

"I almost fired you for letting Mr. Cartwright go into that building alone."

Garrett adjusted his stance and pulled Jules toward him. "We weighed the pros and cons and decided to go with it. I was right there in case anything was botched. Had my eyes on Jesse the entire time."

"I know, I was only kidding about firing you."

Jules wasn't sure he actually was based on the stern look on his face, but she' didn't say a word. Instead, she chose to snuggle up into Garrett's side, never wanting to leave it again.

"By the way, we caught another man who Jesse was working on this operation with. We found him waiting in a dark colored van down the street from here. He had no problem talking and told us a lot of information unlike the other asshole who destroyed Jules' apartment."

Her apartment. She'd almost forgotten about it given how far they'd come since the incident that started it all.

"Are we on the hunt for anyone else?" Garrett voiced the thoughts she was having to herself out loud.

"As far as we know, no."

Jules closed her eyes and let her head hang back, allowing her face to be softly caressed by the soft breeze that was blowing. It really was over.

JULES WALKED across the threshold and smiled at the first thing that greeted her: a photo of a smiling West family hanging in the hallway.

Garrett closed the door behind her. "That's my mom's doing I assure you."

Jules looked slightly over her shoulder at Garrett. "It was very sweet of her to do so."

"Can't deny that. She took care of organizing my move while we were staying in the safe house. I'll probably be shifting things around for a few weeks, but I can't complain."

She heard Garrett take a step toward her and he wrapped his arms around her from behind. Feeling him encompass her in his arms made her feel warm and cozy in this new environment. "Thanks for bringing me here."

"Of course."

Garrett offered to drive her back to her parents' home once they'd been cleared to leave the scene. She declined, adding that she wanted to go somewhere that didn't seem tainted by the ordeal she'd just faced, and he offered to bring her to his brand-new apartment.

"I think I'm going to move too."

"Oh yeah?" Garrett turned her around gently so that she was now facing him.

"Yeah, I've been debating it off and on since the evening that everything occurred, but it's a done deal. At least in my mind now. I can't go back to living there."

"That's understandable."

The two stared at each other for a moment, neither one daring to say a word that might ruin this time between the two of them. There was still so much that needed to be said, yet neither one of them was willing to make the first move.

"How about I show you around first? I, at the very least, know the floor plan, but can't guarantee what is actually in each room."

Jules chuckled under her breath and looked down at Garrett's outstretched hand. The small gesture made her think that the conversation they needed to have would go well, even if they were both stalling before the inevitable needed to happen.

She slipped her hand into his bigger one and allowed him to lead her across the space, enjoying exploring it not just for the first time herself, but seeing some of the excitement he expressed when he came across his things in the space. She could never imagine moving into a place without being there to direct where things went, but Garrett didn't seem to mind.

Garrett showed her the entire apartment before leading her to the living room. "You know if my mom hadn't helped me move in, I would have bribed Flint to at least set up my television and make sure I had a couch. The rest could have come later."

Jules couldn't help but giggle and knew he meant it. It also reminded her of how he had slept on the couch in the safe house while she took the bedroom. Thoughts of the chat they needed to have resurfaced and she said, "You know we need to talk, right?"

Garrett nodded. "Yes, but first, do you want anything to eat or drink? I can assume we have water, but I'm not sure what food is available. Take a seat and I'll go check. If there isn't anything in here, I'll order takeout."

"A glass of water would be great." Her mouth would very likely get dry due to nerves. She could feel it doing so now in anticipation of what might come about as a result of them talking.

Garrett soon handed her a glass of water and she watched as he sat down to order takeout for the two of them. Although

Gladys had made sure that there was food in the apartment, Garrett decided neither one of them should have to cook and they both agreed on ordering Italian food.

Once that was settled, Garrett took her right hand in his left and Jules stared at their union, hoping the words that were about to flow out of her mouth would be enough to save what they were building before it all came crashing down.

"I want—"

"I'm sorry for—"

The couple chuckled at their desire to say their part to get this conversation going.

"Can I speak first?" Jules asked, and when Garret nodded, she continued, "I overreacted when it came to the news about my brother. I could have handled it better because I know you were stuck in a tough situation. And you were right that it wasn't your story to tell. I'm sorry."

Garrett squeezed her hand. "I know some of that stemmed from our past history, so I can't say that I blame you. I should have told you because I knew it was a big deal given what you've told me about your relationship with your brother in recent years. It would have been easier just to tell you once I had seen where our relationship was going."

Jules' ears perked up at his admission. She slipped her hand out of his and laid her head on his shoulder. "Our relationship? Where did you see it going?"

"I see us spending a lot of time together. Exclusively."

Jules moved her head to look at him. "Are you asking me or telling me?"

She bit her lip as she watched him weighing his options. His eyes danced back and forth between her and the front door of his apartment, which was in the opposite direction of where they were sitting. She tried to stop herself from snorting, but soon a belly laugh followed before their laughter joined together as one.

"I'll say yes, whether it was a question mark or a period at the end of your comment."

His eyes lit up after she spoke and his lips descended on hers, marking her comment with a kiss. Their kiss shifted from airy and light to a more serious kiss before Jules pulled back a little.

"Our food is going to be here soon."

"So? Gives us plenty of time to continue our make-out session." He placed a quick peck on her lips.

"But knowing you, things will turn more serious and then we'll get interrupted."

Garrett weighed what she said in his mind before he sat back in his seat. "Oh, by the way, there's one thing that I'm going to do as soon as you get some rest."

"What's that?'

"Take you out on a date."

26

"Don't you dare," she said teasingly. Jules looked up at Garrett's reflection in the mirror. He was standing several feet behind her as she was putting her makeup on in the mirror. She could see the gleam in his eye that told her what he was thinking.

"What?"

"I know exactly what you're thinking, and we don't have enough time to do that before we need to leave."

"I still have no idea what you're talking about." Garrett took a step toward her.

"And you're full of shit."

He chuckled and took another step forward.

"Garrett..."

She intentionally planned ahead and made sure they had plenty of time to get ready for the arrival of the town car that would be taking them to the Cartwright Foundation Gala.

Jules was so happy that even with everything that had happened to her and her family over the last several weeks, the foundation's employees and the event planning team had worked long hours to pull the event together. Pictures of the setup had been sent to her and she loved how everything had turned out. The decor was classy and were variations of the colors gold and red. The seating arrangements were created so that the event looked formal which fit perfectly with what the foundation was trying to show: the achievements that were reached this year and fundraise for the goals they wanted to hit next year.

HER THOUGHTS about the gala were interrupted when she felt Garrett's warm hands on her shoulders. Her bare skin erupted into goosebumps that she couldn't attribute to the physical temperature in the room. No, it was all due to him.

"We can break in your new apartment."

That caused Jules to burst into a fit of giggles. "Break in?" She was surprised she was able to get the words out due to how hard she was laughing. When she was able to calm down, she focused on looking at how sleek she'd been able to get her hair. If she had any say in it, her hair was going to look perfect tonight.

Garrett chuckled and shook his head. "That's one of the things I love about you."

Jules stopped examining her hair and looked at him again in the mirror. "That's one of the things you love about me?"

Garrett just shrugged before grinning at her in the mirror. "That's what I said. I love you." He took another step toward her.

"Do you want to know what I love about you?"

"What's that?"

Jules looked down before she looked back at Garrett in

the mirror. "Your ability to make me feel as if I'm at home no matter where we are. Plus, you constantly keep me on my toes including right now. I love you too."

Garrett took another step toward her and turned her around. He tilted her face toward his with a brush of his finger before his lips met hers.

"Don't mess up my hair. It took a long time to get it to look like this."

"The last thing I'm thinking about is your hair."

"I know and that's the problem."

Jules had intentionally not finished putting on her makeup because of the heated glances Garrett kept throwing her way. She was proud of her quick thinking which would allow for this detour without being late for the event.

His fingertips grazed the straps of her tank top, teasing her. "You know that we're going to have to get a move on here soon. The town car will be here any minute."

Garrett gently nibbled at her lips before he whispered, "I know that's not true. We have plenty of time."

He took a step back and reached down to pick her up, eliciting a squeal from her lips. He carried her through the apartment she had moved into the previous week and was still slowly pulling it together. The couple ended up in her bedroom, where he gently tossed her on the bed. She had to admit that she landed pretty gracefully on the surface given the circumstances. He rid himself of the white shirt that he had thrown on after they woke up and stalked toward her. Instead of climbing on the bed, he took a moment just to stare at her, but his expression wasn't unreadable. In it shined love and affection with a hint of what was about to come. Without a second thought, his body soon covered hers and he was leaning down to kiss her once more.

Jules' hand moved down to his gray sweatpants, and she gently ran a hand along his waistband before trying to get her hand down his pants.

"Patience..." he said as he thwarted her plans when he lowered her tank top and took one of her nipples into his mouth.

Jules moaned in delight as her hands made their way into his hair. She could feel him grow harder and she couldn't help but smile to herself. She was so happy she hadn't put on a bra yet.

His teasing drove her toward her limit, and she wondered if he could drive her to completion just by doing that.

"Are you ready for me?" he asked just before he switched nipples.

"I think you know the answer to that," she responded breathlessly.

"I still want to see how patient you can be."

He alternated between her breasts, and Jules closed her eyes, enjoying the sensations that he was driving through her body.

"How are you doing this to me and not going mad yourself?"

Garrett paused his movements and looked into her eyes. "Because I love pleasuring you."

Jules couldn't help the emotion that she experienced at his simple words because she felt the same. He crawled back up to her and planted a kiss on her lips. She had no problem letting him slip his tongue between her lips, enjoying the way that his kiss made her feel.

He pulled away yet remained only half a breath apart. "There's something I want to do."

Jules' heart skipped a beat. "What's that?"

"I want you to ride me, beautiful."

"But—"

"Try not to overthink it," he said as he moved down her body. When he made his way with her panties and pajama shorts, he stepped off the bed and removed his own pants, showing that he had nothing underneath.

Jules reached over and grabbed a condom that Garrett had placed on the bedside table the night before and flung it on the bed, not caring where it landed.

Garrett climbed back over and kissed her before rolling them both over, her on top of him.

"I want to see you take control."

"I—"

His kiss halted any thoughts she had of proceeding with what she almost said. Jules felt around briefly for the condom before she moved back, putting it on him, and watched him through her peripheral vision. As she lowered herself down onto him, he groaned, not only showing his approval but his arousal. Only when she felt his fingertips graze the sides of her waist, did she start to move.

"Fuck," rushed out of his mouth, and she grinned and took it as a sign to move faster. "You don't know what this view is doing to me."

"I can hazard a guess," she said, her words flying out in quick spurts because she wanted to save all of her energy for the task at hand. Having him under her, with her in control was a brand-new experience, one she wouldn't soon forget.

Here, she controlled the tempo and set the pace and as a result, she could see that she was driving him wild.

That, in turn, made her feel even more powerful.

"You're going to need to speed up here."

Jules smirked. "I thought it was my turn to set the rhythm."

"Yes, and while I'm enjoying it, I want to make sure that you're satisfied before we have to get cleaned up again."

As much as she hated to admit it. He did have a great point. Her smile deepened and she started moving faster. In addition to her speeding up, Garrett met her every move, dragging them both closer to the climax they knew was coming. Jules reached out and used the headboard as leverage, not having a care in the world other than getting them the bliss they so desperately craved. When she reached the point of no return, Jules closed her eyes and let the explosion of ecstasy flow behind her eyelids and throughout her body. She didn't stop moving until Garrett followed her over the cliff. Only then did she collapse on top of him.

The two were completely silent other than letting the sounds of them attempting to catch their breaths do the talking.

Garrett laid a kiss on her head. "Your hair looks pretty good."

Jules bit back a cuss. She almost forgot about the gala. She quickly sat up and ran her hands over her hair, hoping to smooth out the flyaway wisps of hair. "We definitely need to get a move on it. I think we might just have time for another quick shower."

"We definitely do if we take one together."

"Deal." Jules stood up and stretched, but before she could

walk to the bathroom, she said, "Well, we might have just pissed off my new neighbors."

"Hopefully not, but if so, we had fun doing it."

Jules laughed again and snuggled deeper into Garrett's arms.

No matter where they were, they knew that as long as they had one another. That was their happy place, their salvation from any storm that they faced.

EPILOGUE

J ules leaned over and whispered in Garrett's ear, "Aren't you happy you decided to come out with us tonight?"

"I'm not sure what I had in mind about what tonight would be, but I don't think this was it."

Jules snickered as she watched her friends sitting around the table. She did a little shimmy in her seat when the chorus of 'Livin' on a Prayer' came back in before she replied, "If you'd been around when we were younger, you would have run away as fast as you could. This is all of us in a more settled down state."

"Speak for yourself."

Jules didn't react to Liv's comment, but Eve rolled her eyes, giving Liv the ammunition she needed to continue. She'd already been on a roll, complaining about her lack of dates recently.

"You know what? This group has to be cursed."

"What are you getting at, Liv?" Rae chimed in from her spot next to Flint. The group was once again gathered at the

Green Hat, and there was now an extra seat at the table due to Garrett's addition to the group.

They'd been at the Green Hat for the better part of an hour, and everyone had drinks in front of them. This was one of the rare evenings that Flint was able to join the group thanks to not having any political obligations that night, and Rae couldn't have looked any happier. That was why Jules assumed she was only five minutes late this evening.

"First of all, every time I look around, someone in this group is getting into trouble, whether it's their fault or not. And now all of you guys are in loving relationships and it makes me want to barf. On the other hand, though, you all will keep my business booming, so do as you will."

The table laughed as Liv stuck out her tongue much like a child would do. Jules blushed when Garrett looked at her. Marriage hadn't been something that they talked about, but she'd hoped they were on the path leading there.

"Now you know you just probably just jinxed yourself, right?"

"No, I didn't. I don't believe in superstitions anyway."

"You're a wedding planner…who doesn't believe in love."

"Oh, I believe in love. I just haven't found that person for me. Besides, I take pride in my job to convince my brides nothing will go wrong on their big day. Has nothing to do with whether or not I believe in love, however."

Eve sighed. "She has a good point. Okay, Liv, you won this battle."

Liv gave a thumbs up before the group laughed and chatted amongst each other, happy to be together once more. Jules leaned over and rested her head on Garrett's shoulder, enjoying just being next to him while out with her friends. He placed a kiss on the top of her head, and she smiled.

After everything that had happened to her, she could finally say she was happy in all facets of her life. She had a loving relationship and friendships that she cherished. Her immediate family was doing well, being supportive of her recovery, as well as her mother accepting Sebastian's job choice.

The Cartwrights had decided not to press charges on Jesse and pushed to help him get the mental care that he needed. William offered to pay for all of his expenses as long as he promised to try to move on with his life and never harm anyone again. Taking care of Marie had drained most of his and hers funds, so he was unable to pay for the help he needed and that was another reason why William offered to step in and help. So far, the deal had been working and Jules couldn't be happier for everyone involved.

When Jules moved her head and turned back to look at Liv, the smile vanished from her face. "Liv, what's wrong?"

Her friend was staring down at her phone with a concerned look on her face. No one else at the table noticed the interaction besides Garrett since he was sitting in between Jules and Liv. Liv didn't respond to Jules' question, so she called her name.

Liv looked at Jules and said, "Hmm?"

"Is everything alright?"

"Of course it is. Why wouldn't it be?"

Jules could tell that Liv was keeping something from her but didn't want to ask too many questions in such a public place. In fact, she didn't get an opportunity to because Liv was already in the process of leaving her seat. "Where are you going?"

"I need to grab something from my office for a bride. Work never stops, am I right?"

"But it's 7:00 p.m. on a Monday."

"This is what happens when you decide to go out on your own and run your own business. Or so I keep telling myself. I hate that I'm cutting this short."

Liv walked over and said goodbye to the couples and Jules shared a look with Garrett. It looked as if he didn't believe the story she was telling either.

"I'll talk to you all later, okay?" She threw a few bills on the table. "And have another round on me."

Just as quickly as the look of concern appeared on her face, she was gone.

Pre-order Sabotage in the Capitol Today!

SNEAK PEEK OF SABOTAGE IN THE CAPITOL

The smile that had been on Liv's face morphed quickly into one of concern as she read the text message that appeared on her phone.

Kelsey: Liv, we need you back here at the office as soon as possible.

Liv: What's going on?

Kelsey: It'll be easier to explain in person. You're going to want to see this.

"Liv, what's wrong?"

Liv looked at Jules and said, "Hmm?"

"Is everything alright?"

"Of course it is. Why wouldn't it be?"

Jules' eyes narrowed, and Liv could see the questions forming, but she didn't have time to explain. Nor did she have any information to explain yet, anyway.

"I need to grab something from my office for a bride. Work never stops, am I right?"

"But it's 7:00 p.m. on a Monday."

"This is what happens when you decide to go out on your

own and run your own business. Or so I keep telling myself. I hate that I'm cutting this short."

Liv quickly said goodbye to her friends before throwing some money on the table, intending to cover the alcohol that she'd drank while she was there. She knew she'd over paid and would probably get some change back, but she didn't care. She needed to get out of there because Kelsey's text message was alarming.

Liv gathered her things and walked out of the Green Hat, hoping that the quickness in her step would get her back to her office faster.

She thought it might take too long to call for a car, so she flagged down a cab and hopped into the car immediately. Once she gave him her destination, she sat back trying to calm her rapidly beating heart.

Liv had hired Kelsey a few months ago when she branched out on her own and started her own wedding planning business from the ground up. Over the last few months, she'd gotten to know Kelsey, who was a hard worker and made it a point to remain calm no matter the circumstance. The fact that she was freaked out about this spoke volumes in Liv's mind.

She pulled out her phone and quickly called Kelsey, hoping to find out more about what she had seen before Liv arrived. When Kelsey's phone went to voicemail, Liv freaked out, thinking that something might have happened to her.

No matter the situation, Liv tried to find the bright side of a situation, no matter how dark things seemed. At least that's what she tried to do since she moved to D.C. years ago. There wasn't anything bright about what she could potentially be walking into right now.

Liv tried calling Kelsey again, but she still didn't respond. The only good thing about this situation right now was that Liv was almost at her office, so she'd hopefully find Kelsey soon enough.

When the cab driver pulled to a stop outside of her office, he turned to her just as she was handing him the cash for the ride. "Does something smell like smoke to you?"

It took a second for Liv to realize that he was right; something did smell smokey to her. "Yeah, I hope it's nothing serious. Keep the change."

He thanked her as she was getting out of the car. She quickly walked up the stairs and entered the town home that she was renting as office space for her business. She found Kelsey in the living room of the townhome that now doubled as a waiting area.

"Kelsey, you're alright. I tried calling you, but you didn't pick up your phone. I was worried."

"I'm so sorry. I've been trying to figure out who could have done this." She pointed behind her and Liv found what looked to be a wedding dress in a protective bag.

It wasn't the oddest thing to be in a wedding planner's office that was for sure. "Were we expecting a wedding dress to be delivered here?" Although Liv was pretty sure she knew the answer to this, she wanted Kelsey to verify.

"No. And you might want to take a look at it."

Liv raised an eyebrow at her before she walked over to the protective cover and unzipped it. She gasped and took a small step back when she found an expensive gown based on the name brand completely destroyed. It was shredded into pieces. Who would do such a thing?

"Kelsey, did this package have an address or phone number on the container it came in?"

"No. I checked for that too but didn't see anything."

A knock on the door brought their conversation to a standstill. Who could it be this late at night? A thought flew through her mind, and she wondered if any of her friends had followed her from the Green Hat here. She quickly glanced at her phone but didn't find a message indicating such.

"Why don't you go and call the police while I go and answer the door?"

"Liv, I'm worried. You need to be careful."

The person knocked again. Liv quickly walked over to one of the windows that was on the same side of the building as the door and peered out. She couldn't see the person who was knocking on the door.

"Stand in front of your desk so that you can have a full view of the doorway. If I'm not back in two minutes or if something happens to me, tell the police."

Kelsey nodded and did as she was told while Liv grabbed her own cell phone and walked to the door. She kicked herself in the butt for not renting a place that had a window that allowed you to peek out to see who might be at your door. She made a point to remind herself to have security cameras installed this week if possible.

"Who is it?"

"Guess."

No. It couldn't be.

With a deep breath, she swung the door open. Her eyes widened and her mouth fell open. She never expected to see her ex-husband again as long as she lived.

"It looks like your past has finally come back to haunt you."

She couldn't manage to get herself to form any words, so he continued.

"Come on now, darling wife. Surprised to see me?"

Pre-order Sabotage in the Capitol Today!

ABOUT THE AUTHOR

B. Ivy Woods has been writing for as long as she can remember. After getting her Bachelor of Arts in Political Science and Environmental Policy and a Master's in Energy Policy and Law degree and working in the environmental field for several years, she decided to become a stay-at-home mom. That is when thoughts of a writing career really took off. Although she competed in NaNoWriMo multiple times, 2019 was the first year that she won. This win inspired her to make writing a career. Her debut novel was self-published in 2020.

Although she is originally from New York City, she currently lives in the DMV (Washington, D.C., Maryland, Virginia) with her husband, daughter, dog, and cat.

www.bivywoods.com